Finding Faith

Jennie's Gifts Book 3

Best Wishes, Lynn

Finding Faith

Jennie's Gifts Book 3

a novel by

LYNN THOMAS

Net Partners Publishing
2014 USA

Copyright

Finding Faith
Jennie's Gifts Book 3

This is a work of fiction. Names, characters, places and incidents are either products of the author's imagination or used fictitiously. Any resemblance to actual persons, living or dead, business establishments, events or locales is entirely coincidental. All trademarks and brand names used in this book are the property of their respective owners.

Published by NetPartnersPublishing.com
Published in the United States of America
2014 Cover Design by: www.StunningBookCovers.com

Print ISBN-13: 978-0692337400
Print ISBN-10: 0692337407

Jennie's Gifts Series

"... a feel-good read in and of itself... filled with spiritual wisdom that will open your heart and lift your soul. We need more books like Jennie's Gifts and more authors like Lynn Thomas." ~ Suzanne Giesemann, Hay House author.

Book 1: Messages of Love and Healing
Book 2: Dancing on Moonbeams
Book 3: Finding Faith

ALSO BY THIS AUTHOR

Forgive and Release
The Dog Who Found Christmas

http://www.LynnThomas.info

Acknowledgements

In grateful acknowledgment of my husband, family, friends and fans for their loving encouragement. Thanks to Tom and Jamey for reading the drafts, to Cindy for her helpful equine knowledge, to Bryan for answering my paramedical questions, and to Joan for helping me bend that darn spoon! Deepest gratitude to the Creative Spirit that inspired this Series. And to all my readers, thank you for reading *Jennie's Gifts* and more. ♥

Dedication

This book is dedicated with love
to Ryan and Jay
and as always to Tom.

CHAPTER ONE

March

I LANDED ON the asphalt with a hard thud that brought me to my senses. I jumped to my feet and ran for refuge at the far end of the sidewalk. Jake joined me there, and when we sat down I noticed he was holding his neck.

"What's wrong?" I asked as blood seeped through the swollen fingers of his hornet stung hand. "Oh my God, were you shot?"

Jake glared at me.

Why hadn't my spirit guides warned me that he could get shot? Had they tried to tell me, but I failed to receive the message? And if they had forewarned me, could I have prevented it?

Jake was about to say something when there was a blinding flash of light followed by a deafening explosion.

"What the heck was that?"

Six Days Earlier

I had been giving more readings in a day than I had booked in a week when I first opened my store last fall. I was feeling tired and cranky from working long hours, and looked forward to my vacation of rest and relaxation when my assistant, Megan, came to my door.

"Adena Higgins is here," Megan said. "She has no appointment, but is asking to see you."

"Adena Higgins? I don't recall that name," I said.

"She's never been here before, but says a friend referred you."

I glanced at the time. I had planned to leave early today, but reluctantly agreed to see her. "Show her in," I said.

Megan returned to my office with Miss Higgins, a beautiful young woman with long red ringlets framing her lovely but angry face. It appeared that something or someone was upsetting her.

Adena ignored my offer for her to take a seat, and instead began pacing the floor. She ranted a good ten minutes, then stopped to grab tissues from the box on my table, and dabbed at her tears. "When will Kevin leave her? That's what I want to know!" she said, and without letting me respond, renewed her pacing rant.

'Shouldn't I say something?' I silently asked Mica, my spirit guide.

"No," Mica said, "let her get it out of her system."

I nodded, acknowledging her advice.

Welcome to my world. My name is Jennie, and I am a professional medium in the small town of Del Vista in Central Florida. I work from my office in my Sunflowers Shoppe, which is located just off the town square. My store opened last fall, and it is where I met the love of my life, Jake Walker.

We married last New Year's Eve and now reside in his house at Del Vista Estates. He manages the pro-shop at the golf course there, and is an avid golfer. I'm not as enthusiastic about the game, but have golfed with him on occasion.

When Jake and I met, he was a widower. He and his first wife, Connie, had no children, but he has been accepted into the family by mine.

I have two adult children from my first marriage to Ben Malone. Our eldest is Kate. She lives an hour away with her two children, Evan and Lola. Our son, Nathan, lives in Portage Lakes, Ohio with his pregnant wife, Bridgette. They have a daughter, Emily, and their soon to be born son will be named Oliver. Unfortunately, the distance from Florida to Ohio makes it difficult to see them as often as I'd like.

During our volatile marriage, Ben was a struggling artist. I tried my best to support his dream, but he cheated on me anyway. He has since found some fame and fortune thanks to his new manager and second wife, Jasmine. They met after our divorce was final, and as much as I hate to admit it, I like her. She is a charming and intelligent woman, and if she wasn't married to my ex, we could have been the best of friends.

My best friend, Deanna Dey, is also a medium. We met during training with Sara Kelsey, a phenomenal mediumship instructor and my mentor. When Sunflowers first opened, Deanna sublet the office across the hall from mine. But she soon found that she didn't like to give readings. She has since used her Gifts to help solve cold cases for the police and private detectives.

I've wondered if I too might be happier solving crimes and working without the confines of an office or set appointments. But I've been too busy with readings to take the time to find out.

Adena spewed a stream of profanities that startled me. Holy cow, that woman's so full of anger she'll never finish her tantrum! Maybe Deanna had the right idea; working cases must be more interesting and rewarding than this.

But I'm likely just suffering from burnout. Time off with Jake was what I needed, and I've looked forward to starting our vacation tomorrow at our cabin in North Georgia.

Adena paused for a breath, but she wasn't done harping. Megan knew I wanted to leave early today, but this wasn't her fault, since I had agreed to see this tiring woman.

I hired Megan last fall as my assistant, and she's also my store manager. She is reliable and proficient, and manages the storefront, our advertising and our inventory. She's told me that she enjoys this job, as it gives her the opportunity to apply what she's learned in both her business major and her art minor. All I know is that I'm grateful she's working with me, as she has proven to be invaluable.

A large oval gray mist appeared in front of Adena. What was that? Was it an entity? Was it a symbol? Whatever it was, it preceded each step and matched her pace as she continued her rant. All I've been able to surmise so far is that her boyfriend's name is Kevin and he's the one she's so angry about. Other than that, I knew nothing about this new client.

As Adena raved, I noticed the silver spoon on my desk. It had become my nemesis during a recent spoon bending workshop I attended with Deanna. Sara Kelsey was the instructor, and when Deanna asked me to go, I said, "What does that have to do with mediumship?"

"It says in Sara's flier that it's about physical mediumship and the manipulation of energy," Deanna had said. "Listed examples of physical mediumship include table tipping, levitation, manifesting apports, and spoon bending."

During the workshop, Sara had said, "Demonstration helps shatter any conditioned limiting beliefs we've placed on the material world. Manipulation of energy reminds us there is more going on than we perceive. Physical mediumship shows that more is available to us than what appears as real. And it helps stretch us into a higher level of what's possible."

That all sounded well and good, but in a class of about fifty students, I was one of three who could not bend a thing. "You're trying too hard," Deanna had said.

That was easy for her to say since she was one of the successful ones. "Expect it to bend and it will," she told me, "have a little faith."

Faith? What did spoon bending have to do with faith? Besides, I had as much faith as anyone in that classroom, didn't I? But ever since that fateful night, I have tried and tried to bend that spoon with no success. It's silly, but that unbent spoon has shaken my self confidence.

As Adena ranted, I picked up the spoon and held it with both hands as Sara had instructed. I focused my attention on the metal twisting while thinking the command to *'Bend! Bend! Bend!'* And as usual, nothing happened.

I tossed the spoon aside and looked at the clock. As much as I appreciated Mica's guidance to be patient with my client, I needed to get home and pack for my trip. Besides, her raging was giving me a headache. It was time I put an end to it.

But just as I was about to speak, she stopped pacing and took her seat across from me at the reading table. She looked decompressed. She grabbed some tissues and blew her nose, then for the first time since she arrived, she acknowledged me with a nod. "So what do you think?" she said.

"What do I think about what?" I said.

"What do you mean about what? What do you think about Kevin!"

CHAPTER TWO

"WELL FROM WHAT I've gathered, Kevin sounds like a liar and a cheat. If that's your opinion of him, why would you want to be with him?"

"Because I love him."

"Oh, I see. Let me ask you, how long have you known Kevin?"

"We'll be together four years next month."

"And in all that time, did you know he was a married man?"

She flinched, but said nothing.

"So what do you want from me?" I asked.

"I want you to tell me *when* he is leaving her!"

"First of all, my business is with you, and by extension your relationship with Kevin. But it is unethical for me to tap into his relationship with his wife."

Adena's eyes flashed with anger, and her skin flushed crimson, but she made no comment. She didn't have to. It was obvious by her reaction that she was used to getting her way, and I wasn't cooperating.

"Four years is a long time to get to know someone. What do *you* think he'll do?"

Adena grew quiet, then said, "I think he'll stay with her."

"And how does that make you feel?"

She sighed, then said, "Used."

"But you knew all along he was a married man."

"Hey, I didn't come here for a lecture!"

"If Kevin left his wife for you, would you trust him?"

"Of course! Why? What do you mean?"

"Well, wouldn't he cheat on you just like he's cheated on her all these years?"

"No, it's different with us. He loves me."

"Oh? And what's with this gray mist clinging to the front of you?"

She looked alarmed. "Where? What is it?"

"I've been wondering that, too," I said, and silently asked for information.

"She's ignoring her gut, and not listening to her intuition," Mica said.

The mist morphed its shape and grew denser. "Oh, it's an oval shaped mirror!" I said, delighted to receive a new symbol.

"A mirror? What are you talking about?"

"Life reflects back to us like a mirror. This symbol tells me that you're not facing reality, and you're ignoring your gut. So, what do you not want to see for your future?"

She looked stunned. "You're the psychic, you tell me."

I shook my head. "No, I won't forecast your future. I'm a medium, not a fortune teller."

"What's the difference?"

"The purpose of mediumship is to uplift and heal the bereaved, and to prove the continuity of life."

"I don't care about any of that! Tell me my future," she said, her face flushed with anger.

"I can't. It's yours to decide with your free will and choices. Your future is up to you."

"Then why am I paying you? You are nothing but a con artist, taking advantage of people and stealing their money!"

"That's quite an accusation!" I said. "I have not conned you in any way. And you have not given me the opportunity to be of service."

She stared at me a beat, then said, "Service? What are you talking about?"

"I never claimed to be a fortune teller. I'm a medium who can connect with your loved ones in spirit."

"But I don't care to hear about dead people."

"Not even from the gentleman standing behind your chair?"

Adena looked around, then back at me. "Stop that! It's creepy. I don't want a dead person around me."

Ignoring her comment, I said, "This spirit communicator is showing me that his hair was once as red as yours, but turned gray with age. That is how you'd remember him. I'm getting his name now." I sliced my hand in the air, feeling my way through the virtual alphabet in front of me. "It's an E, then a D... Is it Edwin?"

Adena looked surprised. "My grandfather's name was Edan."

"Yes, that's it," I said as the spirit nodded. "And he's showing me strawberries, and a farm."

"Grandpa had a berry farm," she said excitedly. "I'd help him there each summer."

I silently asked the spirit for more information. "He is showing me a tractor. It's old and rusty, but he says he never wanted a new one. He liked tinkering with things."

She laughed for the first time since we met. "Yes, and Grandma would get angry he was so handy. She rarely got anything new."

I nodded as I watched the vision unfold. "He's showing me a rocking chair on a porch. He sits in it and holds a child on his lap," I said, zooming in for a closer look. "The child was you. You're watching the sunset. And next to his chair sits a dog with one blue and one brown eye. Your grandfather says you liked that dog."

"You must be talking about Patches, their Australian Shepherd!" she said, then sighed. "I haven't thought of them or their farm in a long time."

"Your grandfather tells me you always had a hot temper, even as a child."

She blushed. “Guess I tend to get a bit emotional.”

A bit? “He says he’s the one who could always calm you down.”

“That’s true, he was so comforting,” she said as tears filled her eyes.

“He says he’s still comforting you.”

“He is?”

“Yes, and he says he understood you because he too was prone to anger.”

“He was? I never knew.”

“That’s why he’d tinker with things, it helped focus and calm his mind. As a child you intuited his kindred nature.”

“What do you mean?” she said.

“You intuitively aligned with him at the energetic level.”

“I’ve never heard anyone talk the way you do. I still don’t get what you mean,” she said.

“It wasn’t something you learned to do, it was what you felt innately.”

“Oh, but why are you telling me this?” she asked.

“Because he wants you to learn to calm yourself.”

“How do I do that?”

“By channeling your energy into something you can be passionate about, and not pursuing what you know in your gut is wrong for you. Your conflicting emotions are causing you great distress.”

“Are you talking about Kevin?” she said.

“Let me ask you, what would your grandfather say about Kevin?”

She flinched.

“That’s what I thought,” I said. “So, you do know what’s best for you.”

“But I get all confused,” she said.

“Your confusion is from the inner conflict of going against your gut and ignoring your intuition. I’d like to make a suggestion that might bring you some clarity.”

“I’m all ears,” she said.

"Journal each day and get all your thoughts and feelings on paper. And write about what you really want in a relationship, and if you're getting it with him. Keep writing until you get clear and calm. You can do this using pen and paper, or typing at your computer. And pay more attention to your gut. Your intuition has been guiding you all along. Distance yourself from that relationship, at least during this process. Keep working your journal, and following your gut to discover your self. When you reach a calmer and more relaxed state, you can intuitively align with a future you'll really want to create," I said.

"So I should stop seeing Kevin?"

"What do you think?"

"I'm embarrassed Grandpa knows about him."

"Well, if you felt in your gut he was good for you, I doubt you'd feel embarrassed. And your grandfather only wants the best for you."

"Well, I guess I can try that journal thing, and try to listen to my gut," she said.

"Don't try, do," I said.

After Adena left, I turned off my laptop and slipped it into its travel bag. I grabbed my purse, cell phone, and that darn silver spoon, then turned off the office lights and closed my door.

I stopped at the front counter to go over a few last minute details with Megan, and said, "Call if you need me."

"I will, and have a good trip," she said.

"Thanks, see you in a week."

When I stepped outside I nearly skipped to my Subaru. I was eager to get home and pack for our vacation. And I looked forward to being in the mountains with nothing to do all week but rest, relax and cuddle with Jake.

CHAPTER THREE

OUR DRIVE UP to Georgia was uneventful, till we reached the town of Blue Ridge and Jake turned in at Mercier Orchards. We ate in their deli, then purchased jam and fresh apples in their store.

On our walk back to the Jeep we spotted the wood carver. Last year we watched him carve a block of wood into an eagle, but today he was resting on a chair, sipping coffee from a mug. “Howdy,” he said as we neared.

“Hello,” we said as we admired his assortment of carved animals and birds on display.

“Last time we were here I asked if you’d like one of these, remember?” Jake said.

“Yes, I remember,” I said.

“Well, would you like to get one for our cabin?”

The tall bear was impressive, but I felt drawn to the small rabbit, and said, “That one.”

“Sure you don’t want the bear?”

“I’m sure,” I said.

Jake paid for the hand carved wooden bunny, then crammed it into the packed Jeep. “I’m glad you didn’t want that bear now.”

“Oh, why’s that?”

“I wouldn’t have gotten it in the Jeep!”

☼

When we reached the cabin, it felt good to be home. Jake turned the water on and checked the utilities, while I set the wooden bunny near the front door. It made a good doorstop.

We unpacked while we aired out the cabin, then drove to town for groceries. We were both so tired after our long day, that we ate a light dinner, then went straight to bed

☼

"Will you go to Gainesville with me?" Jake asked when he woke me.

I cuddled into him, enjoying the closeness. But the last thing I wanted was to take another long ride so soon after our drive up here yesterday. "Will you be terribly offended if I stayed here?" I said.

"No, I'd like you to be with me, but I understand. No worries."

As he started to get off the bed I grabbed his arm. "Don't you want to cuddle some more?"

"It's tempting," he said as he jumped to his feet, "but I have too much to do."

While I had looked forward to coming here, to lounge around and enjoy the change of pace and scenery, Jake's mission had been different from mine. His was to tend to some repairs, and get the place ready for summer. He had inherited this lakefront cabin from his parents, and tried to visit it at least once per season. But we hadn't been here since last Thanksgiving.

☼

After breakfast, Jake started his shopping list while I loaded the dishwasher. He walked out to the dock and I dashed upstairs to take a shower. As I toweled off, a weather alert interrupted the music on the radio, warning that we were in for a violent rainstorm. I better tell Jake.

I dressed in jeans and a pullover sweater. My wardrobe here in the mountains was quite different from what I wore in the tropics, and I enjoyed that change of pace too. I walked up to the front window and saw Jake standing on the dock using a tape measure and writing on a pad of paper. My man sure looked sexy dressed in his jeans, boots and huggable flannel shirt.

A flock of geese soared across our cove, parallel to the shoreline. They flew in formation, gliding a few feet above the surface of the water, before disappearing around the bend.

There was so much natural beauty here. I liked the contrast of the red clay banks with the dark brown barks and the varying shades of evergreens. And we were fortunate to have a view of forestry land rather than of other houses.

I was in the kitchen refilling my coffee cup when Jake walked in and said, “Are you sure you won’t go with me? There’s a lot of great shops and restaurants in Gainesville. We could go out to eat.”

“Thanks, but I really just want to put my feet up and read a book.”

“All right, I’ll get back as fast as I can. And I'll grab some takeout for dinner on my way home.”

“You mean I don’t even have to cook?”

“Nope, you can just relax,” he said.

“Sounds good, oh, and be careful. They announced on the radio that we’re in for severe weather.”

“I’m always careful, but it’s going to take several hours. It’ll be getting dark by the time I get back.”

“Do you really have to go? Can’t you just stay here with me?” I asked as I hugged him.

“Mighty tempting, and I’ll be expecting more than a welcome home kiss when I return, so rest up.”

"You can count on it," I said as I followed him to the front door. He walked out to the Jeep, and I waved goodbye to him as he drove away.

I walked back to the kitchen for my cup of coffee, and carried it with a book to the living room. I set the cup on the table, stretched out on the sofa, and was tucking an afghan across my lap when my cell phone rang. I looked at the caller ID, and answered it. "Hi, Deanna."

"Hi, Jennie. How's Georgia?" she said.

"How did you know we were at the cabin?"

"Megan told me when I called your store this morning."

"Well, Jake asked if I wanted to come along while he does his spring chores."

"I doubt it took much coaxing."

"No, it didn't. It's so lovely here, and we're already seeing signs of spring."

"And you'll be there for a week?"

"Yes, why?"

"I was hoping you'd help me."

"Help you with what?"

"With a missing coed. Her mother called asking for my help."

"Oh? So it's not a cold case?"

"No, and I hope it won't turn into one."

"Well, how can I help?"

"When I heard you were in Georgia I figured it was fate."

"Oh? In what way?"

"The girl lives in North Carolina, not far from where you are. So I hoped you'd go in my place."

"Me?"

"Yes, and I can help you by phone," she said.

I walked over to the front windows and looked out at the lake. A pair of mallards were pecking at our shoreline. On the back deck, pots of daffodils had started to sprout, their tender green tips poking through the top of the soil. I leaned my head against the window pane. All I had really wanted was to rest and relax, and read my book. And I looked forward to a romantic evening tonight with Jake. The wine was already chilling.

"I sense your hesitation," she said, "but please don't say no. Time is of the essence, and we must get started right away."

"I understand, but..."

"Would you at least phone her mother before making your final decision?"

I sighed. How could I possibly say no to a distraught mother? Why had I answered this call? "I can't just leave Jake and drive up to North Carolina. Besides, I've never worked missing persons. I wouldn't know where to begin. Can't you phone someone who is more qualified?"

"You'll do fine. Just tap into spirit like you do for a reading, and follow your guidance."

As I debated saying no, Mica said, "Go."

My shoulders sagged. "What's the mother's phone number?"

"So you'll do it?"

"I guess so."

"Great!" Deanna said, ignoring my lack of enthusiasm. She gave me the phone number, and said, "The woman's name is Paula Mear."

I nearly dropped the phone. "Did you say Mear? Would her husband be Mathias Mear?"

"I don't know, she didn't say. Why? Do you know them?"

"I might," I said.

"That is significant! You must help her now. She may be the real reason you went to Georgia."

"I thought it was to vacation and cuddle with Jake!"

"Looks like the spirits had other plans," she said, and hung up.

I stared at the phone number a minute, then dialed it. When a woman answered I said, "Is this Paula Mear?"

"Yes," she said.

"Would you by any chance also be Paula Peters?"

She hesitated, then said, "Who is this?"

"My name is Jennie Walker, but you knew me as Jennifer Schwin."

"Good heavens! Jennie? Is it really you? It's been years! How are you?"

"I'm good. So you're a Mear now? Did you marry Mathias?" I asked as the memory of my high school crush came to mind.

"Yes, I did. And how about you, are you married?"

"Yes, but I'm afraid this isn't a social call."

"Oh? Then why have you called?"

"I got your number from my friend, Deanna Dey. She asked me to phone you."

"Why would she do that?"

"To help in finding your daughter."

"Oh? I left Deanna Dey a message, and I've been waiting for her to phone me back. Are you saying you're a psychic, too?"

"I'm a medium," I said. The Jennifer she went to school with over thirty years ago would never divulge that.

"You can't be serious! Are you really a medium?"

"Yes, I'm serious."

"Oh, I hope you can help us then. We're worried sick about our Faith."

"Can you tell me what happened?"

"Faith was last seen two nights ago at the campus library. She had been studying with another student who said that Faith left before her. Faith's roommate phoned the police the next morning when she saw that her bed was not slept in.

"The police searched the campus and found Faith's books and her purse in the bushes near the front steps of her residence. Her wallet and cell phone were still in her purse. The police made inquiries, but so far everyone claims they didn't see or hear a thing. How is that possible?"

"Maybe it was too dark out? Or it was so late at night that the other students were already in their rooms?"

"I guess. And everyone tells me to sit tight. But I can't! I have to do something. A friend suggested calling Deanna Dey. She heard about her from a friend of a friend who works at a police department. And you know the rest. So can you help us?"

I hesitated. Should I tell her I had no experience in missing persons? Would that just add to her stress? But as far as I knew, Deanna had only found one missing person; other than that she had focused on cold cases. But that didn't matter. This wasn't about Deanna; it was about me. *'Am I up to the challenge?'*

"Yes," Mica said.

For Paula's sake, I hoped Mica was right. I'd have to trust and rely on my guides more than ever. But I wanted to be upfront with my friend.

"To be honest, Paula, I've never worked a missing persons before. But I'm willing to help."

"Well, I've never dealt with anything paranormal before, but I'm desperate enough to try anything. Where are you now?"

"I'm in North Georgia. How far is that from you?"

"About two hundred miles," she said, and gave me her address.

I entered the information into my phone, and its navigational app pinpointed her location. It looked like mountain mileage was going to take longer to drive than the same miles in Florida's flat land.

"Okay, I'll leave shortly and will see you soon."

After we disconnected, I phoned Jake, but got his voicemail. I left a message that I was driving to North Carolina to help old friends find their daughter, and that I would explain later.

I ran upstairs to pack some things into my satchel, then grabbed the bag and my purse on my way downstairs. I stopped at the front door, longing to stay here, but knowing I had to help Paula.

After locking the door I walked up to Jake's old Toyota Land Cruiser. He had nicknamed the classic vehicle TLC, and kept it stored here year round. I've never driven it before and hoped TLC would get me to Paula's house.

I slid onto the seat and tossed my purse and satchel on the passenger seat. My unbent spoon tumbled out, and said, "I'll bend you yet!" as I set it on the dashboard.

Jake hadn't started TLC in months, so I held my breath as I turned the key. I was mighty grateful when the engine started. I studied the gauges a moment, hoping I had enough fuel to get me there and back.

It's been years since I've driven a manual transmission, but as I grabbed hold of the stick shift my muscle memory kicked in and I backed it out of the driveway. As I moved the stick into first gear, I imagined a white light of protection surrounding me and the vehicle, then shifted my way down the street.

And so I was on a new adventure. But instead of waiting on Jake or going to Gainesville with him, I was now alone, heading away from him. What had I just gotten myself into?

CHAPTER FOUR

I FELT REMORSE for the way I had abandoned Jake. If I had waited, he probably would have driven to North Carolina with me. But I couldn't wait if it meant a delay in finding Faith. He'll understand, won't he?

As I drove along the highway, the sky ahead grew dark and ominous. Within a mile, I went through a curtain of rain, and into the belly of the storm the radio had warned about. Its intensity increased the higher I climbed in elevation.

TLC shouldered its way against the strong gusting wind, and its wipers worked at a frantic pace. It was now difficult to see through the pelting rain. And as much as I'd like an updated weather report, I switched off the radio since I couldn't hear anything over the deafening storm.

My hands gripped the steering wheel, and I could barely see more than a car length ahead of me. I hoped that if I came up behind another vehicle, it would have its lights on. So far this had been a desolate stretch of highway.

There was a thunderous boom as lightning lit up the sky, and reflected on the spoon resting on the dashboard. My nemesis was an omen, my faith was being tested. Sara said during the workshop that things happen according to our beliefs and expectations. What were mine?

Hadn't I expected my spoon to bend the same as my classmates who had succeeded? Did this reveal some remnant of doubt perhaps stemming from childhood? I was raised to cloak my Gifts so as to not upset my mother. I realize now she meant no harm, she simply feared what she didn't understand. But her fear had programmed me to disown my abilities.

I've since worked at letting my light shine, but this spoon showed that I still held something back. Did it have to do with the visions I've had of past lives where I was persecuted for my abilities? Had I embedded fears from past lifetimes into this one? Regardless, I'd have to rely on my guidance and intuition for Paula's sake. I better trust those Gifts now.

Paula and I were friends in high school. Not the best of friends, but we were in some of the same classes, and social circles. After graduation, I moved to Florida with my parents, and she moved to North Carolina with hers. We lost touch till now, till fate, till Faith had reunited us.

Would I recognize Paula? Will she look the same? Did she know that Mathias and I dated while in school?

And would Mathias, who had been our school's star quarterback, remember that he broke my heart when he stopped calling me? At the time, I was quite distraught. Then one day a mutual friend told me, "Mathias stopped dating you because he wasn't getting any."

I was so naive, I asked, "He's not getting any what?"

"Sex," the friend said. "He isn't getting any sex from you, so he's moved on."

Had Paula given him the sex I wouldn't? Did he date her right after me? I couldn't remember. And what did it matter? This journey wasn't a class reunion.

And as for Jake, he'll understand my need to rush to a friend's aide, right? Even a friend I haven't seen in over thirty years?

It was my call of service. And as Mica was always quick to remind me, my Gifts weren't about me, or always called on at my convenience.

Another flash of lightning and a loud boom of thunder echoed in the mountains. As I rounded a bend, I came up behind a long creeping semi truck. There was no way I'd risk passing this big rig in this low visibility. Better to just follow its red tail lights like a beacon up the hill.

As we crested the top I hoped my brakes would hold out down the steep incline. I down shifted and kept tapping my brakes so as not to run into the back of the truck. I made note of each runaway truck ramp sign, just in case I needed to pull off. It was then that I lost cell service. I just hoped I wouldn't need it.

The road leveled off in another mile, and a flash of lightning illuminated an exit sign just as my phone sprang to life and its app told me to take the next right. I did so, and at the stop sign, I looked both ways twice before turning left. The narrow road was a steep twisting ride, and I prayed I wouldn't come upon a washed out section of pavement.

I reached the peak, and my phone again fell silent as I coasted down the hill to another stop sign. With no bars, no service, and no friendly voice navigator, I tried to recall the final turn, and took a left.

I drove about a half mile when the pavement gave way to dirt. This didn't feel right. The country lane narrowed, barely wide enough for TLC. If another vehicle came my way, there wouldn't be room to pass each other or turn around. And I didn't relish the idea of backing my way out of here.

This can't be the way to Paula's house, as I was driving into denser forest. At least the rain had decreased, which helped in my search for a place to turn around. In a quarter mile I found such a spot, though it was just wide enough to make a tight multi point turn. I was grateful when TLC was finally turned around without falling into a ditch or ramming a tree. Eager to get out of there, I drove as fast as I dared.

When I exited the forest, TLC's tires gripped the pavement. I sped past the familiar stop sign, and came upon my first mailbox, then another. There was quite a distance between the rural driveways, but at least I was in a neighborhood.

As I approached each driveway, I looked for Paula's house number. When I rounded a bend the house numbers jumped to a new sequence. How could I have missed her house?

I turned around and carefully noted each mailbox again before returning to the stop sign. I turned left and drove up the hill searching for service. When my phone displayed bars, I pulled onto the berm and called Paula.

"I can't find your house," I said when she answered.

"When you get to the stop sign turn right. Our house will be on the left."

"I tried that, but didn't find your house number. Where exactly are you?"

"Oh, I should have warned you about that. The numbers on the left will go from 101 to 111 then jump to 601. But if you keep going you'll find us at 115. Don't ask me to explain the numbering system, because I can't," she said.

"You also failed to mention there's no cell service in your valley," I said a bit tersely, feeling stressed. "I was relying on my phone's navigation."

"Sorry," she said. "I'll go turn the porch light on so you can find us."

"That would be helpful," I said as we disconnected. Why hadn't she already turned it on?

The rain had stopped with only the occasional lightning flash in the distant sky. But the early evening hour had already turned dark. I didn't know if it was because there was no moon, cloudy sky, or being in the deep valley, but it was pitch black out here.

I turned around and drove back to the stop sign, again losing cell service. I turned right and drove past 101, 103, 105, 107, 109, 111 on the left. I came to 601, then 603, 605, 113 and there it was, 115.

A woman waved at me from the porch as I drove down the long grassy driveway. Must be the place. As I parked TLC she walked out to greet me. When she drew near, I noticed that she carried a bit more weight on her once reed thin frame. And her long locks were now streaked with gray. But I knew those eyes and that smile anywhere.

I gave thanks for my safe arrival, then grabbed my purse and satchel, shoved the spoon in my pocket, and stepped from the Toyota. As we met each other, she swatted away my handshake, and gave me a friendly hug.

"It's so good to see you again, Jennie," she said. "Thank you for coming."

I felt a nudge at my leg, and looked down into the dark warm eyes of a beautiful collie looking up at me.

"That's Duke," she said. "He's nosy, but friendly. Don't worry, he won't bite."

"It's nice to meet you, Duke," I said as I patted his head. He wagged his tail in response, then led us to a door at the side of the house. As soon as Paula opened it, Duke rushed past us inside.

We stepped into the kitchen, and I was surprised to see how expansive the interior of the house was. From the outside the place looked deceptively small and plain. But it was a lovely place, with high ceilings, hardwood floors, an updated kitchen, and a cozy living room. And Duke warming himself in front of the large stone fireplace made the homey atmosphere complete.

"You can stow your things there for now," Paula said as she pointed at the hall tree. As I did so, I heard her say, "Do you remember Jennie?"

I turned around and saw Mathias standing next to Paula. He was a bit heavier and his hair had grayed. But this was unmistakably the rugged, good-looking guy I had lusted for in high school. It felt a bit awkward standing here amidst Mathias and Paula, but he showed no trace of recognition as he looked at me.

"Nice to meet you," he said.

Was he serious? Did he really not remember me, and that we had dated?

"Mathias, that's a fine way to greet an old friend," Paula said with a slap to his shoulder.

"What do you mean?" he asked, backing away from us.

"Don't you remember Jennifer Schwin? She went to our high school," Paula said.

CHAPTER FIVE

MATHIAS SHRUGGED, SHOOK his head and said, "No, sorry, I don't recall."

Paula waved her hand dismissively at him as he left the room. "Take no offense, Jennie. Sometimes I think he forgets who I am."

"It's fine," I said.

"Make yourself comfortable," Paula said as she led me to the living room.

"If you don't mind, I'd like to see Faith's bedroom."

"Of course," she said, "come with me."

I followed her upstairs, and saw three doors off a long hallway. Paula opened the first door on the right and said, "This was our eldest daughter Joy's room. She moved to New York with her fiancé last year, so I turned it into my sewing room."

From her tone, she either didn't approve of her future son-in-law, or that Joy had moved so far away. Maybe it was both. In the center of the large room was a spacious work table, a computer with a printer, and two sewing machines. The walls held racks of quilts in various stages of completion.

"As you can see, I'm really into quilting," she said.

"They are beautiful," I said as I marveled at her handiwork. If this was just a social visit, I would have liked to linger there and discuss her patterns and techniques. Instead, I followed Paula out of the room.

"This is the upstairs bathroom," she said as she opened the door and flipped on the light. The walls were pink, decorated with hand-painted flowers. I traced one of the petals with my fingertip as Paula said, "Faith painted those freestyle."

"She's quite talented," I said.

"Yes, she is," she said. We walked to the end of the hall where Paula opened the last door. "This is Faith's bedroom."

The walls were a soft yellow, hand painted with daisies in a tangle of green vines along the walls and the ceiling.

"My father would not have allowed me to paint on his walls," I said. "She's lucky that you encourage her creativity."

Paula smiled proudly. "Faith has loved to paint since she was a child. She's majoring in art," she said, then sighed. "With Joy moving away and Faith living on campus, our house has felt empty. Mathias keeps asking Faith to come back home and commute to school like Joy did." Paula sat on the bed, pulled a tissue from her pocket and dabbed her tears.

I walked over to the dresser and picked up a hairbrush. I stroked the soft bristles with my thumb, and asked, "Is this Faith's brush?"

"Yes," she said.

With brush in hand I circled the room. Lightning flashed outside, bringing my attention to the window. As it again lit up the sky, it illuminated TLC parked in the driveway.

"I need to phone my husband. He's probably trying to call my cell. Do you have a phone I can use?"

"Of course, call him from here," she said as she pointed at a telephone on the nightstand by Faith's bed. "I'll go brew us some tea."

"Don't bother on my account."

"It's no bother; besides, I need to keep busy."

Paula closed the door behind her. I sat on Faith's bed and noticed a photograph next to the telephone. I picked up the frame for a closer look. The girl reminded me of Paula from years ago, complete with her long, thick, reddish-brown hair. Faith stood next to a guy with deep chocolate eyes. They were standing in front of a waterfall, hugging and smiling. And she was wearing a gold heart shaped locket around her neck.

I set the frame on the nightstand, and phoned Jake.

"Hello?" Jake said.

"It's Jennie."

"My God, I've been worried sick! Why haven't you answered your cell?"

"There's no service here."

"I was about to call the hospitals! Are you okay?"

"Yes, I'm fine."

"I can't believe you drove to North Carolina... alone and in this heavy rain. Why didn't you wait for me to go with you?"

"I needed to leave right away. Besides, you said you had a lot of chores to do."

His anger was palpable. "The chores can wait!" He paused a beat, and sighed with frustration. "Who are these friends, anyway?"

"I went to high school with them. Deanna asked me to help find their daughter."

"I see, but you drove TLC? I haven't checked it in months. Did you have any problems?"

"No, it got me here fine," I said.

"What about the storm? Did you encounter bad weather?"

I chose not to answer that. "Look, I'm sorry if I've upset you, but my friend needed help, and I responded."

"But why would your spirit guides put you in danger? Shouldn't they be protecting you?"

"I'm fine, I'm not in any danger," I said as I bit my lower lip. I didn't want to fight when I already felt so guilty for leaving him.

"Is this a number where I can reach you?"

"Yes, this is the Mear's home number."

"How long will you be there? Do I need to call work to take more time off?"

"I'm not sure yet, but I'll have to get back too for appointments that I don't want to reschedule. Hopefully, I'll be here two nights at the most. I should know more by tomorrow, okay?"

"Okay, but be sure to call me tomorrow with an update."

"Will do."

"And promise me you'll be safe."

"Are you saying that you love me?"

He laughed. "As if you didn't know."

It was good to hear him laugh. "You take care of yourself, too. Be careful working on that dock."

We said love you and good night, and I yawned as I placed the phone in its cradle.

There was a quilt folded at the foot of the bed, which I assumed Paula had sewn for her daughter. I unfolded it, and was delighted to see a pattern of sunflowers.

The sunflower is a symbol of mediumship and of good luck. I needed luck now. I felt tired so I kicked off my shoes, laid on the bed, and tucked the quilt around me. I held Faith's hairbrush as I closed my eyes, and drifted into the realm of lucid dreams.

CHAPTER SIX

I SLIPPED INTO a familiar lucid dream where I was traveling with three astral friends along a highway. We were seated in a self-guided hovercraft that sort of resembled a Nissan Cube, but it had no roof, wheels or steering.

Mitch, as always, sat on the left front seat, with Juliet seated behind him, and next to me. Reno sat on Mitch's right, in front of me. We weren't in each other's incarnations this lifetime, but we were familial in spirit. And we met in the astral realm to help each other with challenges. But we hadn't met in a while, so we had some catching up to do.

When it became my turn to talk, I told them about my trying to bend the spoon, and trying to locate Faith.

Juliet said, "Wow it's all so synchronistic."

"What do you mean?" I asked.

"Trying to bend spoons, needing to trust more in your Gifts, and even the missing girl's name are all about finding faith," she said.

"That hadn't occurred to me," I said.

Reno swiveled his seat to face me, and said, "I agree with Juliet. You have an interesting challenge, Jennie. But first we need to warn you about the hag. Don't acknowledge her if she appears on the median."

"What hag?" I asked as I gazed out at the concrete divider that ran parallel to our lane.

Juliet reddened. "Don't look out there! You might see her."

"What happens if we do?"

"We're not sure," Reno said.

"Then why fear her? And why is she there?" I asked.

Mitch flinched as he turned around in his seat. "It's my fault. I can't get my fearful thoughts of her out of my dreams."

"What has that to do with us?" I asked.

Juliet rolled her eyes. "Don't you remember we help each other with our challenges?"

"Yes, I remember," I said.

"We don't want the hag to loop in with us," Reno said. "So just ignore her. We don't need to know why. Just pay her no attention, and maybe Mitch can release her."

I nodded, and as I glanced out the side window something materialized on the median. The mist took shape and morphed into an old woman. She looked malevolent, as if she stepped out of some nightmarish folklore. She had a large crooked bulbous nose, missing teeth and warts on her face. Strands of long gray hair stuck out from under her black hat, and she wore a black cloak. As we passed she stood up and looked in the window at me.

I quivered with fear.

Juliet noticed my expression and said, "Jennie just looked at the hag!"

"Oops," I said.

"Great! You looped her in with us," Reno said. "Now we're all in her web."

"Not me," I said, "I refuse to fear her."

"Too late," Juliet said.

The car shook violently as it was raised from the pavement toward the sky by an unseen force. I hated to admit it, but I was afraid. With a quick flip, we hung upside down from the vehicle, like bats on the ceiling of a cave.

We screamed with fear as we looked down from this great height at a large body of water beneath us. And with one powerful shake, we were plummeting through the air.

Juliet cursed at me as we descended.

How was this my fault? It was Mitch's fear that brought the hag to us. And this wouldn't have happened if they hadn't told me to not look at her.

I fell into the water and dropped fast toward the abyss. I pushed hard with my legs and clawed my way against the downward draft. My lungs were about to burst by the time I reached the surface. I gasped for air as I looked around to get my bearings. The shore wasn't too far away, so I swam toward it.

When I climbed the embankment, I was surprised to see my grandfather's cottage. He died before my birth, but I knew him from photographs, in dreams and his ghostly visits. I felt a close connection with him, even though I never knew him when he lived in the material version of this lovely place.

And I liked to visit him in the celestial realms, where we sat together on this wide veranda overflowing with plants. It was always just the two of us, sitting side by side, enjoying the expansive view of the lake.

Now eager to see him, I ran up the wooden steps of the cottage, and tried to open the door. But it was locked. I knocked, but there was no answer. I peeked in the windows, but the house was dark. This was unusual. Where could he be?

I ran down the steps and to the side of the house where I looked in the living room window. Embers glowed in the fireplace. On the small table next to Granddad's favorite chair was an ashtray holding his pipe, with smoke billowing from its bowl. I tapped on the window and called out to him, but got no reply.

With a shiver, I woke up.

☼

Where was Granddad and what did this dream have to do with Faith? I folded the quilt back in place, and still clutching the hairbrush, walked downstairs to look for Paula.

I found her and Mathias in the living room, seated next to each other in matching recliner chairs. He stared at the television while she embroidered a quilt.

She glanced up at me, and said, "You must have been tired. I checked in on you, and found you sleeping."

I nodded as I sat on the sofa and said, "In that photo on Faith's nightstand, is that Faith with her boyfriend?"

"Yes, his name is Alfie Westwood. That photo's from when they hiked with friends last summer."

"Is she still dating him?"

"As far as I know." She folded the quilt as she stood up and said, "I'll get you that cup of tea."

Mathias chuckled as he watched the television. I looked around the room, then back at him. Was he really that into the show or just avoiding me? How could he not remember me? We hadn't dated long, but our paths had intertwined, however briefly.

If we had kept dating, would I be the one married to him and living here now? Would I be the one sewing quilts upstairs? Would it be our child who was missing? I pondered the possibility of parallel lives. Was there a clone of him and me living elsewhere along the etheric grid, in a similar dwelling deep in a country hollow with no cell service?

An image of Jake came to mind and my heart filled with joy. I didn't want to be with any other man but Jake Walker in all realms and dimensions.

CHAPTER SEVEN

PAULA RETURNED TO the living room carrying a tray which she placed on the coffee table. From it, she handed me a bowl of stew and a napkin.

"Thought you might be hungry," she said. "We ate earlier."

My stomach growled in response, as I hadn't eaten since breakfast. I ate a spoonful, and it was delicious. When I was done, I placed the empty bowl on the tray and took the cup of tea she had brought me along with a homemade cookie. The chocolate chips melted in my mouth, and I was delighted when she offered me another.

She waited, stirring her tea as I finished eating. She set her spoon on the tray and elbowed Mathias, who picked up on her not so subtle cue to mute the television.

"So Jennie," she said, "how can you help us?"

I had taken a sip of the startling hot brew, and my eyes watered as I swallowed. I coughed, set the cup on the table, and said, "I hope to get clues and information about Faith."

"How do you get this information?" Paula asked.

"I tune in, like a transceiver, to receive symbols and messages from spirits."

"What is that like? Can you give us an example?"

"Sure, I might see a vision, similar to watching a scene in a movie. Or I might hear a voice or any other sound. I might smell a specific odor or feel sensations. And I might just know something, as it pops into my mind. So I'm gathering information and interpreting symbols and impressions using all my senses. During a reading, I first deliver the evidential, then the message."

Mathias stared at me as I spoke, then said, "So how does any of that help us? You work with the dead."

"As I told Paula on the phone, I haven't worked missing persons before, but I hope to help find Faith."

"But I want my girl found and brought home safe and alive!" he said. "I never liked her living away from home. She should stay here and drive to the campus like Joy did."

Paula patted his leg. "Let's not rehash that now, Mathias. We need to find Faith, and Jennie is here to help us," she said to him, then turned to me and said, "Isn't that right, Jennie?"

"I'll give it my best," I said as I thumbed the bristles on the hairbrush. "And I have some questions."

"Go ahead," she said.

"Do you know if she and Alfie had a fight? Did they break up?"

"The police asked us the same thing," she said. "I'd think she'd tell me if they did. The police told me that when they questioned Alfie, he assured them that they were still dating. Why? Do you think he has something to do with her disappearance?"

I shrugged. "I don't know yet," I said.

"I'll kill him!" Mathias shouted so loud I jumped in my seat.

"Now Mathias, we've discussed this," Paula said. "I can't believe Alfie would hurt her. We've known him a long time, and he's always been decent."

"Does Alfie go to school with Faith?" I asked.

"No, he works at the Dream Again Horse Ranch."

"What is that?" I asked.

"The ranch offers trail rides to the public. And it takes in abused, neglected or unwanted horses and tries to find them new homes. Alfie is one of their wranglers, and Faith volunteers there."

I nodded. "Is that where she met him?"

"Yes, she and her friends visited the ranch one day, out of curiosity. A guide was showing them the horses in the paddock when one of the workers rode up to the fence. He jumped off his saddle and walked right up to Faith to introduce himself. He offered to teach her how to ride. She always claimed it was love at first sight."

"Bastard," Mathias said.

Paula said, "I don't want you buying us more trouble, Mathias. The police have cleared Alfie, so leave him alone!"

His face reddened, but he held his tongue. I didn't remember him having a temper back in school, but he was clearly distraught about his daughter.

"Has anyone threatened her?" I asked. "Was she in danger?"

"The police also asked that," she said, then shrugged. "If she has a problem, she hasn't told us."

I swiped the bristles of the hairbrush across my palm and said, "If you don't mind, I'd like to sleep in Faith's room tonight."

"No, I don't mind," Paula said. "The linens are clean and I'll get you a towel and washcloth. Do you need anything else?"

"No, that should be fine," I said, and walked to the front door to collect my satchel and purse.

"We get out to the garden early. What would you like for breakfast?" she asked.

"I don't want to be a bother," I said. "I've brought protein bars, so just a cup of coffee will do."

"Okay, but if you want something else, let me know," she said.

"Thanks, I will. Well, good night. I'll see you in the morning," I said, "unless I'm working."

"Working?" Paula said.

"Yes, with the spirits," I said.

As I left the room, Mathias snorted and mumbled what sounded like "*Loony*", then un-muted the volume on the TV.

"Pay him no mind," Paula said as she followed me upstairs and into Faith's bedroom. She closed the door behind us and sat on the bed. "I'm curious," she said, "when did you become a medium?"

I sat down with her and said, "I've had paranormal experiences since childhood, but kept it to myself."

Paula nodded, then said, "Well, you obviously embraced it at some point, so tell me about it."

It felt a bit awkward opening up to my school friend. For as long as she had known me, I had kept quiet about my Gifts. Where should I begin?

"I've always had an interest in spirituality and metaphysics. But it wasn't until after my divorce that I began studying mediumship. What struck me from the first class was how loving and inspiring the messages from spirit were. And I liked connecting with the energy of the spiritual realms."

"So it was after your divorce that you became a professional medium?"

"No, not right away. I attended many classes, with no plan to give readings to the public. But an experience at one workshop caused me to first consider it as a career."

"Oh? What happened?" she said.

CHAPTER EIGHT

"I ENROLLED IN a new series of workshops offered by the instructor, Sara Kelsey. I had taken her classes before, but this new one was to be about evidential mediumship."

"You mentioned *evidential* before, what does it mean?"

"It refers to giving *evidence* during a reading. It might be a description of or information from the spirit. This helps the recipient acknowledge the spirit communicator. The evidence given will depend on when or how the recipient, referred to as the sitter, last knew the deceased. For example, if they hadn't seen each other since grade school, the spirit would appear much younger than in a reading for a granddaughter. So the evidential medium will strive to establish evidence before giving the sitter a message."

"Do all psychics work this way?"

"Not all mediums train in it, but I imagine mediums could offer this without labeling it as evidential mediumship. And while all mediums are psychic, not all psychics are mediums."

"Oh? What's the difference?"

"Psychics read the subtle energies around a person. Mediums can work psychically, too, but they also communicate with the spiritual realms. And while psychic work can be tiring, mediumship work can be exhilarating. In fact, some nights I'm so charged with the higher spiritual energies I have trouble falling asleep."

"So in your work as a medium, you give messages and foretell the future?"

"I've always shied away from forecasting the future."

"Why is that?"

"Because I've found foretelling to be based on current circumstances and desires. At any point, one's future path can change due to individual choice and free will."

"I guess that makes sense," Paula said. "So how do you get the messages?"

"I receive using one or more of the five *clairs*. I guess the word is French for *clear*, and each clair corresponds to a physical sense."

"Oh? Can you give me an example?"

"Well *clairaudience* means *clear hearing* any sound psychically. This could be anything. I've heard humming, music, voices, and even a dog's bark. In one reading I heard coins jingling and when I told my client, she said that her husband had a habit of jangling coins in his pocket."

"Wow, I guess that was good evidence!"

"Yes, it was."

"So if clairaudience is hearing," Paula said, "what is sight?"

"*Clairvoyance* is psychically *seeing* something with the eyes or the mind. The medium isn't creating this vision, image or picture with her own thoughts, but rather seeing it as it appears or unfolds. I've even stepped inside a vision."

"Really? What was that like?"

"It's hard to put into words. Imagine stepping into a movie and viewing the scene from the character's perspective."

"That would be amazing!" she said. "What are the other clairs?"

"*Clairgustance* refers to psychic *smell* or *taste*. *Clairsentience* is psychically *sensing* an emotion or a physical sensation. For example, a medium feeling a tightening in his chest, could mean that the deceased suffered a heart attack."

"That would be frightening!"

"Not when you understand what's happening. Once the medium receives the information, the impression releases."

"Okay, so that's all five senses," Paula said, counting on her fingers, "but only four clairs."

"The fifth clair is c*lairomniscience*, and is my favorite. It's a clear sense of *knowing*. It's when a message, an answer, or any thought or idea just pops into your mind. It comes in a flash, as if out of nowhere. It's when you don't know how you know something, but you know that you do."

"That sure is a lot for you to remember," Paula said.

"Well, it's just for reference, you're not trying to use them, other than in practice. During a reading, it just happens. And while some mediums use all the clairs, others are stronger with one or two. Everyone has Gifts and we all communicate and learn in our own way. And something I've found amazing is, a medium's diminished physical sense doesn't necessarily impede the corresponding clair."

"What do you mean?"

"For example, a medium who lacks the physical sense of smell, could still psychically detect scent."

"That is interesting," Paula said.

"Yes, and learning about the clairs gave me an understanding of how the spirits had been communicating with me."

"But how do you *do* it?" she asked.

"It's just something I've done my whole life, but Sara's helped me fine tune the virtual dial for better reception. And prior to her training, I'd sense energy or feelings but not understand what was happening. I've learned to discern when I'm receiving impressions, and knowing how to release them has been empowering."

"That's good," Paula said.

"Yes, and by paying attention to how I receive impressions, and practicing with the clairs has increased my abilities. And it's something anyone can do to improve their intuition. So for example, when I first started receiving impressions, I'd ask myself if I first saw an image or heard a sound. Did I feel the tingling on my arm before I detected a scent? And if I received a new symbol, what did it mean? Such self query helped build my database, and gain confidence in my skills. And with such mindful practice anyone can get better at discerning and relying on their intuition."

"I'll have to try that," Paula said, "but what was that life changing workshop you were going to tell me about?"

"Oh yes, it was at Sara Kelsey's evidential class. When I arrived at the workshop that first night, my stomach was in such a knot of fear, I nearly turned away."

"Why were you so afraid?"

"I feared I wasn't Gifted enough. But after driving all that way, I decided to just monitor the class. So after I signed in and paid my fee, I took a seat at the farthest corner of the room, and scooted the chair snug against the wall. The overhead lighting cast me in shadow, and I felt invisible, certain no one would even know I was there.

"From my secluded spot, I observed my fellow students. We ranged in age from late teens to over eighty, a mix of race, nationality and background, with the women outnumbering the men. As I studied them, a woman walked up to the chair next to mine and pushed it snug against the wall as well. That was when I first met Deanna Dey, but we didn't get a chance to talk, as class had begun."

CHAPTER NINE

"SARA GREETED THE CLASS with great enthusiasm, then began her lecture by reviewing the clairs. But when she said that everyone was going to practice at the podium, her announcement received a collective groan."

Paula said, "I wouldn't have wanted to stand up there, either."

I nodded and said, "I guess it's only natural. Even when Sara assured us it would be fun, no one volunteered to go first. So she said she'd choose someone, and I held my breath as I watched her select her first victim. Imagine my surprise when she pointed at me!"

"Oh, you've got to be kidding!" Paula said.

"No, so much for my being invisible! I quaked with fear as I walked to the front of the room, and when I reached her at the podium I told her I had only come to observe. She nodded, then spun me around to face the class. I grabbed onto the podium so tight, my knuckles turned white and my heart pounded."

Paula laughed and said, "I bet you looked like the proverbial deer in the headlights."

"I imagine so, as I was stunned and wondered what I had gotten myself in to. My fellow students sat attentively, waiting for me to begin. I felt sorry that I was about to disappoint them. Sara asked who I felt drawn to. I stood immobile, wishing to disappear or get teleported out of there. Sara must have sensed my anxiety because she told me to breathe. When I took a deep breath, I relaxed a little, but she asked again who I felt drawn to."

"She wasn't about to let you off the hook," Paula said.

"No, she wasn't," I said. "As I scanned each face in the room, I stopped at a man seated in the center row. I detected a faint glimmer around him, but unlike the other expectant faces, he sat with his eyes cast downward. I pointed at him and Sara told me to call out to him. I said, 'Man in the center of the third row. I see a glimmer around you'. He looked up at me and we made eye contact. Then Sara said, 'What spirit is with him?"

"She really had your feet to the fire!" Paula said.

"Yes, but she told me to relax and trust. But all I had seen was the glimmer of light, so Sara said, 'Ask the spirit to come forward."

"What? I would have run from the room!" Paula said.

"Well, it's good I didn't or I wouldn't be sitting here with you now," I said.

"True enough," she said with a nod, "go on with your story."

"So I focused on the glowing aura and it expanded. This aroused my curiosity enough to silently ask the spirit to appear. And an old man in spirit materialized next to the student's chair."

"Really?" Paula said. "You saw an actual ghost?"

"Yes," I said.

"What happened next?"

"Sara asked me to describe what I saw and then she said she saw him, too. This boosted my confidence, and I told the student about the spirit standing next to his chair. When I said that I thought this was his grandfather, the spirit moved one step up behind the man."

"What does that mean?" Paula said.

"It's one of my symbols," I said. "For me, I see parents standing behind the sitter, and grandparents stand behind them and one step up for each generation. I was happy with what I had accomplished, and turned to leave the podium when Sara asked me which grandfather it was. I recalled sensing a soft or feminine energy when the spirit first appeared, so I said it was his mother's father. Sara nodded in agreement, but..."

"Don't tell me," Paula said, "Sara had more ideas."

"You got it," I said. "She told me to ask the spirit for a message. The grandfather smiled at me and then, I swear, he winked."

"You're joking!" Paula said.

"No, it's true, and it was that wink that proved to me I was really communicating with the spirit and not making him up. I stopped feeling self conscious and relaxed, and my awareness of the other students fell away. It was as if the spirit and I were alone in the classroom . I silently told him I was ready to receive his message. When I delivered it to his grandson, he confirmed it was helpful for a problem he was having. And I was again reminded that spirits are wise and loving. And that their messages can transform not only the sitter, but others in the audience, and the medium as well.

"After class I waited until the last student left so I could speak alone with Sara. I told her that when I first stood at the podium, I had feared I'd not have use of my Gifts. She surprised me when she said, 'Why would you lose your Gifts when they're innately yours?'

"I told her that I lacked her confidence and she said, 'In mediumship we have to trust that the spirit will come forth. There is no prepared speech, and we don't originate the messages. We are the channel, and when we receive the information, we can ask for more.' Then she said, 'Stop worrying. You cannot lose your Gifts, they are yours and you can rely on them.' I laughed when I realized how tuned in Sara had been to my internal drama that evening. It helped me realize that mediumship is a process, and it was the first time I felt inspired to consider becoming a professional medium, but I had one more obstacle."

"What was it?" Paula asked.

"My father," I said.

"But didn't he pass away years ago?" Paula said.

"Yes, but I guess I still sought his permission. And one night soon after that class I dreamt of him and that he approved of my mediumship. So after that, I took my study to a new level, which eventually led to the opening of my store."

"You just gave me chills!" Paula said. "What a brave thing to do."

"The courage comes in the allowing," I said. "If I'm self-conscious or doubtful, I'm not connected to spirit. It's when I step out of fear that I receive. That's also true for intuitive guidance. We must trust and have faith."

Paula's eyes misted, and she said, "I hope you can help us find our Faith."

I nodded and said, "I've asked my guides for their assistance."

"And I've prayed to my guardian angel, but I don't have guides," she said.

"Oh? Why not?"

"Because I'm not a medium," she said.

"I believe everyone has guides; one or more our entire lifetime and specialists who step in based on need."

"Well, since we can use all the help we can get, I ask Faith's guardian angel and any other guides to help us now."

We took a moment to affirm that, then Paula stood up and said good night.

I wished her a good night too, hoping it would be just that.

CHAPTER TEN

I DIALED JAKE from Faith's phone before turning in for the night.

"Hello?" he said.

"I miss you," I said.

"Who's this?"

"Very funny! You forgot me already?"

"I could never forget you, Jen."

"That's nice to hear. Was your day productive?"

"You could say that. I carted all the wood and supplies down to the shore, and got everything ready for the morning. But I have to tell you, this will be a test of my skills."

"I'm sure you're capable," I said.

"Thanks for the vote of confidence, and I hope you're right. It's been awhile since I've laid planking and always under Dad's supervision."

Jake's father had been a carpenter by trade and I imagined he wouldn't miss overseeing Jake's project. "I have no doubt he'll be with you in spirit tomorrow."

"He's gonna be looking over my shoulder? I hope I don't disappoint him. So anything new with you in the last few hours?"

"I had an interesting dream."

"What? How could you have a dream? Are you sleeping on the job?"

I laughed. "Sort of, I took a nap and dreamt of my grandfather's cottage."

"Oh? What about it?"

"There isn't much to tell, but that he wasn't home was odd. Whenever I have that dream, he's always been there, so I don't know what it means."

"I'm sure you'll figure it out. Did you dream anything else?"

"Not that I can remember," I said. There wasn't much else to say, but I was reluctant to hang up. I missed him, and the smell of his cologne. And I've grown used to hugging him as I fell asleep. "The minutes feel like hours when I'm away from you."

"Same here," he said. "Come home tomorrow."

"I'll try."

He yawned, then said, "I better get to sleep. I have a tyrannical taskmaster who expects me to start work at dawn."

"Who's that?"

"Me," he said with a laugh. "I've got a lot of work to do, and I hope to get it all done tomorrow."

"Well, don't overdo it. Promise to be careful."

"I will."

"I love you," I said, then told him what I'd like to be doing with him if we were in bed together right now.

"I'm looking forward to that," he said. "Have a good night."

"Good night," I said, and set the phone in its cradle.

After changing into my pajamas, I crawled into Faith's bed, and tucked her sunflower quilt up and around me. After I turned off the light, I set my intention on finding out about Faith, and that I would recall whatever I learned when I woke up.

☼

I slipped into the hovercraft as it sped along the highway, happy to be reunited with my three astral friends. I told them that I was trying to find Faith.

Reno said, "Okay, but let me remind you to not look at the median."

"Why not?" I asked.

Juliet slapped her forehead with the palm of her hand. "Oh, no, not again," she said. "Just don't look out the window, okay?"

I shrugged. "I guess so, but why?"

"Don't you remember that you looped us into Mitch's fear?" Juliet said.

"I did? When? And what's so scary about the median?"

Mitch turned around to face me and said, "It's not the median, it's her. I can't get the fear of her out of my system."

"Who is she?"

Juliet cringed and said, "Good grief, Jennie, the hag!"

"The hag? What are you talking about?" I asked as I glanced out the side window. On the concrete divider that ran parallel to our lane, sat an old crone who looked like she stepped out of the pages of folklore.

She looked right at me and I was struck with fear as we made eye contact. "Do you mean her?" I asked as I pointed at the window.

Juliet screamed, "Jennie did it again!"

"Again? I've done this before?" I asked.

The hovercraft shook with a violent quake as it lifted toward the sky. I grabbed the seat and door handle as the vehicle flipped. Below us loomed a large body of water and just as I feared what would happen, we tumbled out. We fell through the air and plunged into deep water, sinking fast.

With great effort I paddled upward, broke the surface and swam toward the nearest shore. As I crawled up the embankment, I was delighted to see that it was my grandfather's lawn. I sprinted up the steps of his cottage and knocked on his door. But there was no reply. Where was he?

I ran around to the side of the house and peeked in the windows. It was dark inside except for the lit fireplace and the smoking pipe resting in an ashtray on the coffee table. When I tapped on the window I woke up, rolled onto my side and fell into a deep sleep.

☼

I awoke at first light, trudged into the bathroom, and stood in the shower with my head under the stream. As my mind began to clear there was a knock on the door. I turned off the shower, and said, "Yes?"

It was Mathias, his words muffled by the door.

"I'm sorry, what did you say?"

"Are you done in there?" he said as he spoke louder, "We're on a well and you're using up our water."

Embarrassed, I grabbed my towel and said, "Sorry, I'm done."

"Paula sent me to ask if you want breakfast," he said.

"No, thanks, just the coffee."

"Okay, I'll tell her," he said. "We'll be in the garden."

Why would Paula send him upstairs? Hadn't we discussed breakfast last night? I felt uneasy that he had been outside the door. When I pulled on my robe and opened the door, he was standing there. I gasped as I stepped back.

"Didn't mean to startle you," he said, ogling me.

I pulled my robe tighter.

"You're still beautiful," he said.

"Thanks," I said, feeling vulnerable. As I stepped past him, he grabbed my arm. "Let me go," I said as I pulled away from his grip.

"Sorry," he said, "I just wanted to tell you something."

"What is it?" I said, backing away from him, toward Faith's door.

"I do remember you from school," he said. "I didn't want to admit we had dated in front of the wife. And for the life of me, I can't believe I let you get away. But I was a horny kid back then."

"No problem, it was years ago," I said.

"Maybe so," he said, stepping closer, "but I still have needs. And Paula hasn't been interested for awhile. But you and me, we could be quick, if you get my drift. No one needs to know."

"Stay away from me," I said. He grabbed my arm again and I yanked free. "Get this straight. I am not now, nor will I ever be interested," I said, and ran into Faith's bedroom, locking the door behind me.

My adrenaline was pumping fast as I got dressed. I took a protein bar from my satchel and walked up to the door. I put my ear to it and listened, but heard no sound. I slowly opened it and peeked into the hallway, relieved Mathias wasn't there. I didn't think he'd assault me, but it was obvious that he hoped to get lucky. I best keep on guard.

I tiptoed down the stairs, and saw no one in the living room. When I stepped into the kitchen, the aroma of freshly brewed coffee sent me in search of a mug. I selected one from an assortment hanging under one of the cabinets, and filled it to the rim. I carried the mug up to the large bay window and admired the panoramic view. The back deck looked sunny and inviting, so I slipped on my jacket and walked outside. Duke ran up to greet me.

"Where did you come from?" I asked.

He wagged his tail as I petted his head, then followed me onto the back deck. The deck was large, and the picnic table along with eight Adirondack chairs were all decorated with Faith's ivy design. I chose a seat and Duke sat next to my chair, intently watching me unwrap my protein bar.

"I better not give you any of this," I said. He stared at me while I ate it. When I finished he sniffed the empty wrapper, then walked away and stretched out on the deck for a nap.

As I sipped my coffee, I gazed at their property and the tree lined hillside. They had a lovely place and a view I couldn't appreciate last night in the dark.

Paula waved at me from the garden, and when I waved back I saw Mathias working near her. I felt relieved to have distance between us. I liked it better when he pretended to not remember me.

I tucked the empty cellophane wrapper into my pocket and felt the silver spoon. I pulled it out and absentmindedly twirled it between my fingers. Will I find information about Faith today? Can I find her in my dreams?

Duke looked over at me, and I said, "I have a sense of dread, Duke."

The dog whined in response, then laid his head back on the deck.

I drank the last of my coffee and walked back to the door. Duke didn't follow as I stepped inside. I washed the mug and set it on the drainboard, then walked back upstairs to Faith's bedroom.

I slipped the spoon into my purse, kicked off my shoes and laid on the bed. "Show me how to find Faith," I said as I closed my eyes.

CHAPTER ELEVEN

I SLID INTO the hovercraft as it traveled along the highway, and greeted my three astral friends. I told them that I must find Faith.

Reno said, “Okay, but don’t glance out the window.”

“Wouldn’t it be more helpful if we stopped anticipating Mitch’s hag?” I said.

Juliet waved her hand dismissively at me and said, “Whatever, just don’t look at her.”

“Can’t we just release her?” I asked.

Mitch turned toward me and said, “I can’t! I’ve tried. But I’ve feared her since childhood.”

“Who is she?” I asked.

“I don’t know, but she scares the hell out of me!” Mitch said.

“Just decide she doesn’t scare you anymore, Mitch. Tell yourself she doesn’t exist,” I said. “You are no longer a child. Take control of your mind and choose what to think.”

“I’m trying,” Mitch said, “but she keeps showing up.”

“That’s because you keep dwelling on her,” I said.

“Stop picking on him, Jennie! Mitch can’t help it,” Juliet said.

“But we’re energizing his fears. Let’s stop talking about her to help him forget her. Talking about her keeps her activated," I said, and as I glanced out the window the hag looked back at me. "Shit!"

Juliet flinched, then glared at me. "You looked at her again?"

"Why can't we get past this?" Reno said.

"Let's all agree to not think about the hag from now on," I said as the hovercraft shook in its ascension and flipped over. With one violent convulsion we were all tossed out.

As we fell through the air, Juliet yelled, "But it's not about Mitch's thoughts, it's about his fear."

We fell into the water. Water was a symbol for emotion. Was that what this was about? Was it about Mitch's fears and emotions? Or all of ours?

I sank deeper into the abyss. There had to be a way out of this loop. Was this about more than Mitch's fear? I needed to gain insight.

I kicked my legs as I clawed my way to the surface. I gasped for air as I broke free, then sighted shore and swam to it. When I reached the embankment I crawled up to the lawn, and was surprised to find a horse nibbling grass and clover.

The filly was black with a white star marking on her shoulder. I've never seen a horse here before, not even in my childhood dreams. I left her to her grazing, and ran over to my grandfather's cottage.

I dashed up the steps and knocked on the door. There was no reply, so I ran around to the side of the house and peeked in the windows. The lights were on, the fireplace was lit and Granddad's pipe was smoldering in an ashtray on a table.

I tapped on the window, but received no reply. I ran back to the front porch and pounded as hard as I could on the door, determined to get inside. "Let me in!"

The door swung open, and I stepped inside. I walked up to the fireplace and dried my hair and clothes in front of its warm glow. When I looked back at the table Granddad's pipe was gone.

The sound of a woman's voice coming from another room startled me. "Take a seat, Jennie. I'll be right with you."

I sat at a table that looked like the reading table in my office. A woman entered the room and sat across from me. She looked familiar, but I couldn't place her. As I looked into her eyes I realized who she was, and she was lovely.

She smiled and said, "Yes, I'm her."

"But you don't look anything like a hag now."

"That's because I'm not one. But in my most recent lifetime I was an actress," she said. "My name was Myrna."

"Nice to meet you, Myrna, but why are you scaring my friend?"

"I'm not trying to scare him, I'm trying to make amends. You see, years ago I played the hag in a movie. Your friend was very young when he watched it, and I'm afraid my portrayal frightened him. I'm trying to now be of service to him by shedding light on his deeply rooted fear. Since I was the cause, however unintentional, I've volunteered to help him release it."

"But you're scaring him with this nightmare."

"Nightmares illuminate and offer insight and freedom from the fears that induced them. If Mitch would realize that the hag was just an actress in makeup, he'd let go of the fear."

"Okay, I understand. But what does this have to do with me?"

"He has looped my hag into your group, so I've taken advantage of that to also get your attention."

"Why? What's our connection?"

"It's a spiritual one. You are not alone, there is help being offered. All you have to do is ask," she said with a theatrical wave of her hand. "We are all connected in the great theater of life."

"And where is my grandfather?"

"You wouldn't understand if I told you."

"Try me," I said.

"Okay, he's working on a project in the harmonic field."

She was right, I didn't understand. "But why are you using his cottage?"

"To better draw you near, it's familiar ground."

"There must have been an easier way to contact me."

"Perhaps," Myrna said with a mischievous smile, "but this was so much fun!"

"But why dunk us in the lake?" I asked.

"Oh, that's from a scene in that movie I was in. It has proven helpful, has it not?" Myrna said.

"In what way?"

"In getting your answers. What intention did you set before going to sleep?"

With so much happening I had nearly forgotten. "To get information about finding Faith."

"There, you see," she said with a smile.

"No, I don't see. How has any of this helped?"

"Look around, Jennie. Open your eyes," she said.

Faith's hairbrush materialized on the table. I picked it up and swiped the bristles with my fingertip. "I still don't understand."

"That's because you have been using your brain," she said, pointing at her head. "Use your mind."

"Can't you just tell me? Is Faith alive or dead?"

"Yes," she said.

"Yes?"

"Yes," she said, and nodded.

"How can it be both? Which is it?"

"Open your eyes!" she said, and disappeared.

"My eyes are open!" I said so loudly that I woke myself.

I sat up on the bed. Someone was in the room with me.

CHAPTER TWELVE

I LOOKED PAST the foot of the bed. "Faith? Is that you?"

She came closer. "Yes, please tell my parents I'm okay."

"So you are dead?"

"You of all people should know that answer," she said.

"But what happened to you? Where is your body?"

"Find me, Jennie," she said, and faded from view.

I cringed. I had dreaded this outcome and now felt sick at the thought of telling her parents. In a panic, I sprang from the bed and shoved my things into my satchel. I had to get out of here, and home to Jake.

I grabbed my bag and purse as I left the bedroom, but paused at the top of the stairs. Mathias and Paula were talking about me, their voices drifting up from the kitchen.

"Why is she here if all she's gonna do is sleep?" Mathias said. "There must be something wrong with her. She must be sick or something, cause no healthy woman sleeps as much as she does."

"I'm puzzled too," Paula said, "but be quiet or she'll hear you."

"But that's my point, woman. She can't hear us cause she's sleeping! Ever since she got here she has filled your head with foolish ideas, used up our water and slept!"

"Stop shouting at me, and lower your voice!"

I cleared my throat to alert them I was coming down the stairs. As I stepped into the kitchen, they looked over at me from where they sat at the table.

Paula eyed my satchel and said, "Are you leaving?"

"Yes."

"Then you either have no news, or bad news about Faith," she said.

I nodded and bit my lower lip.

"Which is it, dammit!" Mathias said, and pounded his fist so hard on the table the plates clattered.

I jumped, but forced myself to remain calm as I walked toward the front door. Ignoring my instinct to run out of there, I set my purse and satchel on the hall tree, then walked back to the table and took a seat. "I received a message," I said.

Paula's eyes widened. "About Faith?"

"Yes."

"What is it?" she said.

"Faith wanted me to tell you she's okay."

"What the hell does that mean?" Mathias said.

I looked from Paula's fearful expression to his angry one, and my mouth went dry. I've never before told anyone that their loved one was dead. When I met with clients for their readings, they already knew that.

Paula let out a loud gasp at my long pause and said, "No, Jennie, you must be mistaken. It can't be true!"

"I'm afraid it is," I said, and held her hand as tears filled my eyes. "Faith visited me, I mean her spirit did, and she asked me to tell you she's okay."

Mathias slammed the table again and said, "She's not okay if you're saying my little girl's gone!"

"Are you sure, Jennie?" Paula asked.

I nodded.

"Where is she?" she said. "What happened to her?"

"She didn't tell me," I said, "but if she does, I'll phone you with the information."

"This is a hell of a thing!" Mathias said. He knocked the chair over as he stood up, and walked outside, slamming the door.

Paula wrung her hands and said, "What will I do without my Faith, Jennie? What will I do?"

I stood up, walked over to her and hugged her. "Talk to her, Paula. She'll hear you."

Paula shook her head and said, "No, I best not do that. If she's truly gone, I need to let her rest in peace."

Faith materialized next to her mother, and said, "Tell her I'm here."

"Faith is standing next to you. She can communicate with you," I said.

"But I can't see or hear her!" Paula said, weeping into her hands.

"Do you want me to go?"

Paula looked at me, her face grief stricken. "Please stay if you can help find her. I'll be in my room," she said and ran down the hall to her bedroom.

I eyed the sandwiches Paula had prepared for our lunch. I was hungry, but my stomach was now in a knot. I walked over to the kitchen phone and dialed Jake's cell number.

"Hi, how's it going?" he said when he answered.

"Not good," I said, then told him about Faith.

"I'm so sorry for your friends. What are you going to do now?"

"I'm not sure."

"Another nap might reveal more clues," he said.

"It's possible."

"Maybe you should call Deanna, she might have some advice."

"That's a good idea," I said.

"Well, let me know if you're staying or heading home."

"I will. I miss you."

"I miss you too," he said.

I gathered my purse and satchel and returned to Faith's room. I shut the door, sat on the bed and phoned Deanna.

"Hello?" she said.

"Hi, Deanna, it's Jennie," I said.

"Where are you calling from?"

"The Mear's house line."

"How's it going?"

"Not good," I said, then told her my dreams and Faith appearing. "Any ideas?"

"You know better than to ask someone else to interpret what you get."

"Yes, but I've never been in such a spot. I'm not sure what to do," I said.

She was quiet a moment, then said, "If it were me, I'd visit the hag again and demand more information."

"Jake suggested a nap, too. So as much as I don't want to go through that again, I guess I will."

She laughed and said, "Hey, don't blame us for your weird dreams. Maybe you need to ask better questions. And really pay attention to what she says. Let me know how you do."

"Gee, thanks," I said and hung up.

I kicked off my shoes and laid on the bed, tucking the sunflower quilt around me. "Show me where to find Faith," I said and closed my eyes.

☼

I dropped into the speeding hovercraft, but only two of my astral friends were there. "Where's Reno?" I asked.

"He's awake," Mitch said.

"Oh," I said, then told Juliet and Mitch about seeing Faith's spirit and needing to locate her body.

Juliet said, "Okay, but…"

"I know, you're going to tell me to not look at the hag," I said.

She nodded and smiled, pleased I had remembered.

Then to Mitch I said, "Still can't get the fear of her out of your system?"

He turned in his seat toward me. "No, I guess not," he said, then swiveled forward again.

"It's not his fault, Jennie!" Juliet said, always quick to defend him. "Don't make matters worse by dumping guilt on him."

"That's not my intention, Juliet. And I'm sorry to tell you both this, but I need to find the hag."

"What? Why?" they said in unison.

"She holds my answers. But don't worry, I won't make a habit of this."

Juliet reddened and said, "I don't want to get tossed, dropped and dunked anymore! I want us to unloop, not loop in more!"

"I'm sorry, Juliet, truly I am, but it can't be helped," I said as I looked out the side window. "And there she is, right on time."

The hag sat perched on the median, as if waiting my arrival. She stood up as we made eye contact, and with a wave of her hand the hovercraft raised skyward. We were shaken about, then flipped over and out.

Juliet screamed at me as we tumbled through the air. "This better be the last time, Jennifer!"

CHAPTER THIRTEEN

MY THOUGHTS ECHOED Juliet's words as we descended. But this time I fell, not into a lake, but a deep pond. I swam around to get my bearings.

Giant boulders created a natural retaining wall, and a waterfall cascaded from a cliff at the far end.

In my mediumship I have found water to be either a symbol for emotion, or a physical location. Which was this?

I dove under and swam around, disturbing schools of darting fish. The pond was murky; thick with reeds. Strands of sunlight filtered in from the surface and glistened on an object up ahead.

As I swam closer I saw that the object was a heart shaped locket, like the one in Faith's photo. The necklace floated in the water, its chain caught in the reeds. As I drew near, I saw long strands of auburn hair also entangled in the chain. It was Faith. But where were we?

I swam to the surface and spotted the hag sitting on the rocks, watching me. As I pulled myself out of the water and onto the embankment the hag transformed into the lovely actress. Duke sat next to her as she patted his head.

"Such a nice dog," she said, then folded her hands in her lap, looking mischievous. "Now, what is that saying?" she said while tapping her finger to her chin for dramatic effect. "Oh yeah" she said with a snap of her fingers, "you're getting warmer!"

"You mean I'm getting closer to finding Faith?" I said.

"Well, wasn't that your intention?" she asked.

"Why didn't you just tell me where to find her?"

"Hey, don't blame me; you're the dreamer," she said. "Besides, I have no right to rob your unfoldment."

"What do you mean?"

"You've doubted your Gifts when all you had to do is open your eye."

"Don't you mean my eyes?" I said.

"No," she said pointing at her brow, "your eye. Do I have to spell it out for you? Start using your intuition!"

☼

I awoke with the realization that I had been trying to figure everything out, blinded with doubt that I could be effective in this new challenge. That night at class when I stood at the podium and fear blocked my senses, Sara told me to relax. It was then that I received the loving guidance of spirit. And Sara had assured me that my Gifts were innate and I could rely on them.

But once again I had let fear hinder me because I didn't trust I could find Faith.

I sat up on the bed, and scooted back against the headboard. I closed my eyes and connected with the spiritual realms like I do for a reading, and asked about Faith. I opened my eyes and saw a vision of Faith walking alone in the dark.

As she approached the steps to her dorm, a man grabbed her from behind. He escorted her to a red car where a second man was seated behind the steering wheel. Her assailant pushed her into the back seat and got in next to her.

"Did she know the men?"

"No, but she knew of them," Mica said.

"Was either man Alfie?"

Mica said, "No."

Faith sat in the backseat arguing with the first man as they sped off campus. Their argument escalated, and he struck her with his fist. She went limp. He checked her pulse, then shouted at the driver.

The driver said something back, then drove till he came to a construction site where he stole some concrete blocks and placed them in the trunk. He then drove several miles before veering off onto a dirt road. They sped up the mountain and came to a dead end.

As the driver backed the car around, he grazed paint along a boulder. He parked the car, then looked over the back seat and said something to the other man. They got out of the car and together hoisted Faith to the top of an embankment.

The driver returned to the car to retrieve the cinder blocks and some rope from the trunk. He climbed back up, and they tied her feet to the blocks with the rope. When they slid her into the water, she sank deep enough to be invisible from the surface.

I zoomed in at the men's faces, neither was Alfie. The driver was tall and skinny, the other man was shorter and muscular.

The vision cleared, and I pulled a notebook from my satchel. After I wrote everything down and made a sketch of each man, I felt inspired to go to the horse ranch.

Trained to never ignore a hunch, I put my notebook in my purse, then ran downstairs and out to the garden. Paula wasn't there, but Mathias was knee deep in the plants, hands in the soil.

He stood up as I neared him, and wiped his hands on a rag he pulled from his back pocket. "What's up?"

"Where's Paula?"

"She's in our bedroom. Why?"

"I need to go to the horse ranch."

"What for?"

"I have to see Alfie."

His eyes were full of questions as he looked at me. "What about?"

I shrugged. "Just following a hunch, I'll know more once I get there."

He looked about to comment, shook his head, and said, "Let's go."

"You're busy, I'll ask Paula to go with me."

"She's resting. I'll take you."

Mathias started toward his truck, but I didn't want to be alone with him. He stopped walking and glanced back at me. "We'll get there quicker if you get *in* the truck."

I stood rooted in the garden, unable to decide if I trusted him.

"I can give you directions if you'd rather drive yourself."

I felt a nudge at my back, and took a step forward. "Go," Mica said.

"Okay," I said, "I guess I'll go with you since you know the way."

He stopped at an outdoor spigot to wash his hands, and I caught up with him at his truck. He opened the passenger door for me and I slid in.

☼

We rode in awkward silence till, at last, Mathias exited the highway. He pulled onto a dirt road and drove through a gated entrance where an engraved sign welcomed us onto the ranch. Mathias parked in a visitor's space and without comment, we exited the truck and walked up the wooden steps to the ranch's office.

We stepped inside and a man standing behind the front counter greeted us. I asked to speak to Alfie Westwood. He pressed an intercom and called Alfie to the office.

Within a few minutes, Alfie walked in the door. He was much more handsome in person than in Faith's photograph. He walked up to Mathias and said, "Hi, Mr. Mear. Any news on Faith?"

Mathias reddened, his fists clenched. "Tell us where my daughter is, you son of a bitch!"

Alfie stepped back as I jumped between them. Everyone in the office turned to stare at us as I pushed both hands against Mathias's chest and said, "Stop it, Mathias! He didn't do anything."

Mathias backed off, still glaring at the younger man, as I turned around and said, "Hi, Alfie, I'm Jennie Walker. I'm Paula's friend and I'm helping search for Faith. I hoped you could help me."

"Help you how?" he asked.

"We need two horses," I said, surprised as anyone as the words tumbled from my mouth.

Alfie looked from me to Mathias, who also looked startled by my request. "I'll go saddle the horses," he said. "Wait here. I'll be right back."

As Alfie walked outside, Mathias said, "Why do we need horses?"

"I'm not sure, just following guidance. Oh, and leave Alfie alone."

CHAPTER FOURTEEN

ALFIE CALLED TO us and when we went outside we found him sitting on one horse and holding the reins of two others. He jumped to the ground and handed Mathias the reins to the largest horse. “This is GetBack,” he said.

“Why is he named that?” Mathias asked.

“Don’t stand behind him or you’ll find out,” Alfie said.

Mathias muttered under his breath as he climbed onto the big horse’s saddle.

Alfie offered me the reins to the smallest horse of the trio. I stopped in my tracks when I saw the white star on the filly’s shoulder. This was the horse in my dream!

Alfie, misinterpreting my hesitation, said, “Don’t worry, she won’t hurt you. She’s the gentlest horse on the ranch. Her name is Bella’s Star, but we just call her Star.”

“Hello, Star, it’s nice to meet you,” I said as I patted her forehead. With some trepidation I walked to her side. I hadn’t ridden in years, would I remember how? Alfie held the reins while I set my left foot in the stirrup and with some difficulty reached for the saddle horn with my left hand.

I grabbed hold of the back of the saddle with my right hand, and tried to hoist myself up. But Star moved away from me and I had to hop on my right foot to keep up with her.

Alfie walked up next to me and snugged the reins while I tried again, but I couldn't keep my balance.

Mathias chuckled. I guess he found my difficulty humorous.

"Try grabbing Star's mane with your left hand and the horn with your right," Alfie said.

I tried this and was able to stand in the stirrup, but unable to swing my right leg over the saddle. By now I feared injury more than embarrassment, and stepped away from the horse.

Alfie said, "If you don't mind, Ma'am, I'll help you."

"I don't mind," I said.

He stepped behind me, and hoisted me up onto the saddle.

"Thank you," I said, pleased to at last be seated atop Star. But the height made me a bit dizzy, and I clutched the horn.

As Alfie handed me the reins he took notice of my white knuckled grip. "Relax. I promise you, Star is very gentle. Faith always chooses her for our rides."

I nodded, and took a breath. Once I relaxed I was pleased to not only be sitting on the horse from my dream, but that she was Faith's favorite ride as well.

Alfie mounted his horse again, and asked, "Where do you want to go?"

"I'm not sure," I said as I held the reins waiting for guidance.

Star pulled the reins from my hands with her head, making it clear she wanted to take the lead. I let her and as she stepped forward I glanced back at Alfie and Mathias and said, "Follow us."

"Where to?" Mathias said.

"I have no idea," I said as Star took off at a lively gallop across the pasture. She slowed her pace as we entered the woods. The path inclined, and we rode several minutes before exiting onto a dirt road. Was something or someone guiding Star?

Star veered sharply at a fork and trotted up a steeper road. After a mile or so, we came to a dead end. Star stopped, pawed at the ground, shook her head and snorted.

"You brought us all this way to come to a dead end?" Mathias said.

I motioned for him to be quiet. "Hear that?" I said.

"Sounds like a waterfall," Mathias said.

I stood in the stirrups to get a better view. From this height I saw a wall of boulders beyond some bushes. I carefully slid off the saddle, then took a moment to thank Star.

The horse pawed at the ground and snorted again.

Mathias snorted too, and made another "*Loony*" comment under his breath.

I ignored him as I pushed through the bushes, and came to the wall of boulders. The roar of the waterfall grew louder as I climbed to the top of the embankment for a better view. And there was the waterfall at the far end, cascading into the pond just like in my dream!

A glimmer of light appeared on the opposite side of the pond. As I watched, the shimmer grew and morphed into Faith. She looked at me, pointed at the water in front of where she sat, and disappeared.

I climbed down and pushed my way back through the bushes.

"What's going on?" Mathias asked, still sitting on GetBack.

"Just a minute," I said, and ran around the base of the embankment toward the waterfall. There were no bushes here, and there was a smudge of red paint on one of the rocks. As I scurried up the boulders, I was careful to not touch the paint. When I reached the top, I was standing where Faith's ghost had been.

I knelt and peered into the water, but it was too murky to see into its depths. I tentatively slid my hand beneath the surface and closed my eyes. My fingertips tingled. I laid on my stomach, my face just above the water, and shaded my eyes from the sunlight with my hands. There was something shiny bobbing below. I called down to Mathias and Alfie. They brought the horses around, and looked up at me.

"What is it?" Alfie said.

"Call the police," I said. "Faith is... was here."

Alfie dialed 911 as I slid down the wall.

Mathias jumped down from his horse and grabbed my arm. "What's up there?" he said.

I pulled free from his grip and said, "Let's just wait for the police."

"Why?" he said, but I didn't answer him. What could I say?

I ran over to Bella's Star and hugged her neck. Her eyes looked so sad. I spoke soothing words and petted her, hoping to comfort her as she helped to ground me.

We tied off the horses and Mathias started climbing up the rocks.

"Please don't go up there," I said, "we don't want to disturb anything."

Mathias stopped mid-climb and looked down at me. "Tell me what's up there. Is it my girl?"

I feared what he'd do if I told him it was and instead pleaded with him. "Please wait, Mathias. Let the police sort it out."

Alfie turned pale and started trembling.

"You okay?" I asked as I ran over to him.

He stood bent over, hugging his stomach. "I feel sick. I've been here with Faith."

When Mathias heard that he jumped to the ground and ran up to Alfie, his fist raised, ready to strike the younger man.

I screamed, "Mathias, stop! Alfie did nothing wrong!"

"Nothing wrong? He admitted that he brought my daughter here!" Mathias said, then to Alfie he said, "What did you do to her?"

Alfie put his hands up defensively, as he backed away. "I don't want to fight you, Mr. Mear, and I swear I didn't hurt her!"

"Stop, Mathias," I said as I rushed at him, and bounced off. It was like slamming into a wall. But at least I caused him to stagger back a step or two. As I rubbed my now sore shoulder, I said, "Stop jumping to conclusions!"

Mathias gazed down at me, and said, "You better explain things quick, psychic lady, cause Alfie's about to become one of those ghosts you claim to talk to."

"Alfie did not and would not harm Faith," I said.

"How can you be so sure?" he said.

"You just have to trust me," I said, then turned to Alfie and said, "When were you here last with Faith?"

"About a week ago," he said as he kicked at the ground.

"And with Bella's Star?"

He nodded. "Faith liked to ride here."

I looked back at the high boulders. The area was secluded, but that outcropping offered a vantage point. "Did anyone ever see you here?"

Alfie flinched. "Not that I know of."

"What would they have seen?" Mathias said. He resembled a big bear ready to strike. While Alfie had youth on his side, Mathias looked stronger, and was taller and pumped with adrenaline.

I wished the police would hurry up and get here before Mathias did something he'd regret.

Faith materialized next to us and said, "Make them stop fighting!"

'*How do I do that?*' I silently asked her.

I received her answer, took a deep breath to muster my courage, and said, "Mathias, I can assure you that Alfie would not harm Faith."

He looked surprised. "How can you be so sure?"

"Because their in love and plan to marry," I said.

Both men looked startled.

"What did you just say?" Mathias said.

"How do you know that?" Alfie asked me. Then to Mathias he said, "I don't know how Jennie knows that, Mr. Mear, but it's true. Faith and I have plans to tell you and her mother this weekend. I would never harm Faith, I love her. She's my best friend and all I want is to spend the rest of my life with her."

Mathias staggered away, Alfie slumped against a tree, and Faith faded from view. The two men kept their distance, but the tension was palpable. I feared that if the police didn't show up soon, they'd either pounce each other, or dive into that pond to start their own search.

And while I was relieved to have found Faith, I felt trepidation at facing the police. How would they react to my saying I was a medium? Should I tell them it was the spirits and the horse that led me here?

And after I'm done here, I'll have to face Paula with this dreadful news. While we weren't the best of friends, I cared about her and felt great empathy for her as a mother.

I walked back to Bella's Star and leaned against her, finding comfort in her presence while we waited.

CHAPTER FIFTEEN

AT LONG LAST, two police cars arrived followed by a Ford sedan. A detective stepped out of the sedan and walked up to me. Mathias and Alfie joined us as he identified himself as Detective Wick.

"Can someone tell me what's going on here?" Wick said.

"I'll try," I said. "There's a body in that pond."

"And who would that be?" he asked.

Mathias and Alfie sucked in breath as I said, "I believe it's Faith Mear."

"Do you mean the missing coed?"

I nodded. "Yes, this is Faith's father, Mathias Mear and her fiancé, Alfie Westwood."

"Her fiancé? First time I've heard she's engaged."

"News to me, too," Mathias said.

"We're making the announcement this weekend," Alfie said.

Wick made a note on his pad, then looked at me and said, "And you are?"

"I'm Jennifer Walker, a friend of Faith's mother."

"And what makes you think she's in that pond?"

I cleared my throat and said, "I was led here. I'm a medium."

He took off his sunglasses as he scrutinized me. "You don't say," he said.

I nodded, but made no comment. What would Deanna have told him?

He put his sunglasses back on as he wrote another note, then asked, "Has anyone disturbed the area?"

"I climbed to the top of the embankment when we first arrived, but other than that we've been awaiting your arrival," I said.

"I climbed up halfway, but stopped," Mathias said.

"And did you disturb anything?"

"No, I don't think we did," I said as Alfie and Mathias shook their heads no.

Wick pointed at a van that had arrived and said, "Our divers will be in the water shortly. I'll need for all of you to wait here."

Wick walked over and spoke with the officers who had been securing the area. He then walked over to the van. A man and a woman were donning wet suits. They all glanced over at us as they spoke, then we watched as the trio climbed the embankment.

The divers slipped into the pond while the detective surveyed the surrounding surface. One of the divers shouted up at Wick, who nodded in response. The detective reached down and took something from the diver. When he stood up, the gold heart shaped locket dangled from his hand.

It all felt so surreal. Alfie fell to his knees at the sight of the necklace, and Mathias doubled over as if someone had punched him in the gut. "It can't be," he said, and kept repeating it like a mantra.

I rushed to console Mathias, but he pushed me away. I ran over to Alfie and sat on the ground next to him. He looked stunned.

Wick came down to the ground, and we stood up as he walked toward us. We circled him as he showed us the necklace. "Was this hers?"

The three of us stared at the glistening locket. We all nodded, and Alfie said, "I gave that to her. Our photos should be inside it."

Wick nodded as he slipped it into an evidence pouch.

"Can I have it?" Alfie asked.

"Not yet," Wick said.

Another van arrived and as its crime scene technicians photographed and walked the area, a memory triggered in my dazed mind.

"You'll find red paint on one of the boulders," I said. "It's from the car."

"What car?" Wick said.

"The car that brought her here," I said.

He stared at me a moment, then said, "We need to talk, so don't go anywhere." Then to all three of us, he said, "Wait here."

As Wick walked away, Mathias started ranting about what he'd do to who did this, while Alfie sat on the ground in a daze.

An ambulance arrived next and three men got out. I assumed the one not in uniform was the coroner. He walked with a posture of authority as he spoke with the officers. He then climbed the embankment, and knelt to speak with the divers. The two EMTs hauled a stretcher up with them as they scaled the wall.

After much deliberation, the body was pulled from the water. The coroner briefly examined it, then the EMTs hoisted it onto the stretcher and lowered it to the ground.

The divers climbed down as the crime scene investigators climbed up to gather more evidence. The coroner stood talking to Wick, and said something that caused the detective to look back at us.

After, what seemed an eternity, Wick walked up to Mathias and said, "Will you identify the body?"

Mathias nodded and solemnly followed Wick to the ambulance. The coroner spoke with Mathias, then showed him the body. The big man's knees buckled, and the EMTs rushed to his aide. It was disconcerting to watch the Papa Bear deflate like that. I was grateful that Paula wasn't here.

And I didn't want to be here either. I needed to be with Jake. It was all so surreal, yet too real. I no longer wondered if I'd be happier working cases like Deanna. This was not for me. I'll leave the missing and cold cases to her. I'd much rather sit with clients seated in the comfort of my office, giving messages from loved ones they knew had passed.

Wick escorted Mathias back to us as the ambulance sped away. Mathias sat on the ground and Wick called Alfie aside to question him. Mathias looked to be in shock, sapped of energy, and ten years older.

Wick returned with Alfie, and asked me to come with him. "Okay now, tell me how you knew the Mear's girl was in the pond," he said.

What should I say? Do I tell him about my dreams of the hovercraft and the shape-shifting hag? Do I tell him about Bella's Star eating clover on my grandfather's lawn, or that the horse knew to bring me here? What about my vision of seeing Faith in the water, or sensing her energy with my hands? Should I tell him I saw her spirit on top of the embankment? What would he believe?

I handed him a business card and said, "Like I told you, I'm a medium and I was guided here."

He read my card and said, "You're a long way from Florida, Ms. Walker."

"I was vacationing in North Georgia with my husband when Faith's mother asked for help. Paula and I went to school together."

He pocketed my card and said, "Any other guidance, hunches or impressions I should know about?"

"Yes, there were two men."

"Oh? And where did you see them?"

"In a vision," I said.

He hesitated, then said, "Can you describe them?"

"Yes, one was tall and thin, the other short and muscular. They grabbed her from behind and shoved her into a red car."

"Oh, yes, you mentioned that red car before. What make and model was it?"

I shrugged. "I don't know."

"Anything else?" Wick said.

"Yes," I said, "she was in the backseat with the muscular one, and they were arguing about something. He punched her and she went limp. It looked like he broke her neck."

Wick raised an eyebrow, looking surprised by my remark. "Go on," he said.

"I don't think he meant to kill her. It was a heat of the moment kind of thing."

"Anything else?" he said.

"Yes, contrary to Mathias's suspicions, neither man was Alfie."

"I see," he said, then handed me his business card. "If you get any more information, call me."

"I will," I said.

"And it would be helpful if you could meet with our sketch artist," he said.

I nodded, then said, "Oh, I nearly forgot." I pulled my notepad from my purse and flipped through it. "I made these drawings earlier," I said as I pulled the pages from the pad and handed them to him.

Wick looked over the sketches I had drawn earlier of the two men and said, "This is very helpful, thank you."

I don't know what he thought about mediums, but at least he had been courteous. "Can you give me a ride?" I asked.

"Where to?"

"Back to Paula's house for my car. I'd like to get back to Georgia."

"Sure, I need to talk to Faith's mother anyway," he said, then walked away.

I went over to Bella's Star, hugged her neck and petted her muzzle. "I'm sorry, Star," I said, "I bet you sensed something had happened, and I imagine you miss her."

I walked over to Alfie and said, "Can I leave Star in your care? I've hitched a ride with the detective."

"Sure," he said.

"I'm sorry, Alfie. Take care of yourself," I said, and hugged him.

His large luminous eyes conveyed all he was unable to say.

As I walked past Mathias, he glanced up at me and asked, "Where are you going?"

"The detective's giving me a lift back to your house."

He jumped to his feet, brushing loose grass from his pants. "What about the horses?"

"Alfie's agreed to take Star with him," I said, and walked away without offering him a hug goodbye.

I walked up to Wick's sedan and waited while he talked to the techs. He opened the door for me, and I slid onto the front passenger seat.

Mathias ran up to Wick and said, "Can you drive me to the horse ranch? I need to get my truck."

"Sure, hop in," Wick said.

"But what about GetBack?" I asked.

Mathias glared at me and said, "Alfie can handle the horses."

"He can ride with three of them?" I said as he got into the back seat.

"He can manage," Mathias said, "but you could stay and help him."

CHAPTER SIXTEEN

WICK DROVE US to the horse ranch, and Mathias jumped out as soon as he stopped the car. As Mathias climbed into his truck, the detective said, "I fear Mr. Mear is making plans."

"What do you mean?"

"He needs to leave the investigation to us. If he turns vigilante, like I suspect he's planning, those guys won't need a trial; but he will."

I nodded in agreement, and as Wick followed Mathias home, I didn't envy his job of breaking the news to Paula.

Mathias pulled into his driveway and Wick parked behind him. The detective ran from the sedan to catch up with Mathias, and they entered the house together.

They didn't need me to join in, so I walked up to the back porch, and sat in one of the Adirondack chairs. I was staring at the distant hill, when I felt a nudge at my leg. Duke was standing next to my chair. I petted his head and said, "We found Faith, Duke."

He whined and pawed at my shoe, then stood at rigid attention when we heard Paula's scream. The dog and I both quivered at her heart-wrenching wail.

Duke looked at the house, then at me and whined. He took a step forward, hesitated, then stopped. He paced back and forth, his ears twitching at the sound of the distressed voices coming from the house. The dog was tense, anxious and in obvious stress.

"Come here, Duke."

He stood next to me, his body rigid. As I petted the dog, I spoke to him in a soothing voice. And I found it comforting to be with him.

Duke relaxed enough to sit down, next to my chair. He leaned toward me and placed a paw on my leg. I looked up at the colors in the setting sky, while the dog kept watch on the house.

☼

It was dark by the time Wick stepped out of the house. The back porch light came on as he stepped onto the deck, and sat in a chair next to mine. Duke greeted the detective, and he took his time petting the dog.

"Does it get any easier?" I asked.

He glanced at me, then back at the dog. When he didn't answer, I didn't think he would, then he said, "No, it doesn't." He petted Duke a bit more, then said goodbye.

I watched as he backed his car out to the street, then drive away. I wanted to leave, too, but first I had to see Paula.

"I guess it's time to go inside, Duke," I said. But Duke stayed on the porch as I walked toward the house. Mustering my courage, I opened the door and stepped inside.

☼

Paula and Mathias sat together on the sofa in the living room. She wept in his arms as he stoically held her. But his tense jaw belied his calm exterior, his raging emotions were quite palpable.

When I stepped into the room, Paula grabbed my hand. Her face was full of anguish as she looked up at me and said, "Why would God do this to us?"

Paula's words knocked the wind out of me, and I fell into a chair. Her daughter's passing weighed heavily on me, and it felt like the walls were closing in. Not only had I found her body, I had clairvoyantly witnessed her death. I had no experience or training for any of that, and I hadn't expected Paula to say this. It was difficult to be dispassionate.

But I'm not one who believes in a vengeful God that takes a life on a whim or as punishment. And since working as a medium, I have come to view people more as spiritual beings, who remain spiritual beings during and after each incarnation. Birth and death are doorways, and our spiritual essence is eternal.

But I'm not immune to grief. I have experienced the physical loss of my grandparents, my parents and my son-in-law. But I don't blame any of those deaths on a capricious deity.

But this wasn't the best time to discuss my views with Paula. And as she wept, I felt an innate desire to alleviate her grief and take on her burdened heart. As an empath, I have to be careful of the tendency to absorb from others. This has been a problem for me since childhood, especially with my mother.

There is a danger in being too empathic. And the older I get, the harder it has become to bounce back from what I do absorb. I've learned the hard way that it's not a healthy thing to do. It's best to stay dispassionate, and ask the spiritual realms to assist the person.

I took a deep breath, calmed my mind and emotions as best I could, and silently asked how to help Paula.

"Speak from your heart," Mica said.

I planted both feet on the floor to ground myself into the Earth, while I mentally reached for the stars. This psychic stretch brought me into energetic alignment. I looked at my friend and said, "I'm very sorry, Paula."

Her face reddened, pinched with grief as she looked at me. "How long have you known?" she said. "Did you know last night? Have you known all along?"

Her accusations threw me off balance again. "No, I didn't," I said. It's true, I hadn't known, but I had suspected.

"But you must have," she said, "how else could you have found her?"

"I was led one step at a time, guided by my dreams, visions and intuition."

"Is that why you've been sleeping so much?" she asked as she wiped at her tears.

"Yes," I said.

She mulled that over, then looked at Mathias and said, "How do we tell Joy?" Not waiting for his answer, she fell back into his arms and sobbed while he mutely stared into space.

It didn't take a psychic to figure out what he was plotting. I needed to get out of there and away from him. I stood up and said, "If you need to talk, please call me."

Neither she nor Mathias responded as I left the room. I ran upstairs for my satchel. When I walked back downstairs, I stepped back into the living room.

Paula had stopped sobbing, and they both sat in shocked silence.

"Can I call someone to come be with you?" I asked.

"No," Paula said, without looking at me.

"Faith's spirit lives on, Paula. Please know she is okay."

She looked at me. "Go away! Get out of here, Jennie!"

Her words stung. I walked to the front door, and as I opened it Duke slipped in. I watched the dog walk to the fireplace and curl up on the rug before I closed the door.

☼

I felt relieved to be out of there and back in TLC. I patted its dashboard as I pulled onto the road. I drove to the familiar stop sign and took a left. My cell phone sprang to life, finding service as I drove up the hill. The navigational app told me to turn around.

I pulled off onto the berm and entered a new destination. After recalculating, the app corrected course and instructed me to turn right in five hundred yards.

I placed a call to Jake, but it went to voicemail. "I'm coming home," I said, "but I have a stop to make first."

I disconnected and tossed the phone on the passenger seat, then settled in as I headed north, in the opposite direction of my husband.

CHAPTER SEVENTEEN

I LONGED TO go home to Jake, but I was on a mission, and had to trust my intuition.

Within an hour of driving narrow, twisting roads and making numerous turns, my phone directed me to my final turn. I exited the paved road and drove onto the dirt road, past the familiar arched entrance, and parked in one of the guest spots. Being so late at night, the front office was closed, so I disregarded the visitor's check-in notice, and walked straight to the barn.

The inside of the barn was dimly lit, with stalls along each side. As I walked down the long hallway, some of the horses looked out and followed me with their eyes. The majority had their eyes closed, sleeping soundly as I walked past them.

I felt drawn to the last stall on the right, and stopped at it to sneak a peek. A man was inside, standing with his back to me and balancing a dark brown horse's hoof on his knee.

As he examined it, he said, "I don't understand why Garth trimmed your foot so short, Vigor. It's no wonder your gait was off, but the turpentine has helped."

It was him! I stepped up to the opening and said, "Hi, Alfie."

Both he and the horse looked at me. Alfie lowered the horse's foot to the ground and said, "Jennie? What are you doing here?"

"Thought I'd drop by on my way to Georgia."

He frowned as he walked up to the door, took off his hat, scratched his head and said, "I'd say you've driven a far bit out of your way."

He had seen through my charade. "I confess, you're right," I said. "I wanted to see how you were doing."

He shrugged, his handsome eyes full of sorrow. We stood in awkward silence.

"Did you have any trouble getting the three horses back here on your own?" I asked.

"No trouble," he said as he twirled his hat, looking down at the ground. "I told the boss about Faith, and he told me to take a few days off. But I prefer to keep busy," he said, and looked at me. "I can't believe Faith's really gone. It's like I'm in a bad dream and can't wake up."

"It can't be easy. I'm so sorry."

He didn't comment as he donned his hat. He walked over to a shelf and picked up a brush, then brushed the horse, a bit too brisk in my opinion. But Vigor didn't seem to mind.

"Shouldn't he be sleeping? It's kind of late to be grooming him, isn't it?"

"Vigor likes it, and I didn't get to my chores earlier."

"You want to talk about what happened?"

"No, not really," he said.

Mica said, "Just be present for him."

Alfie tossed the brush back on the shelf, then opened the door and led Vigor into the hallway. I followed them to an indoor arena, where he let the horse free, and closed the gate. We watched the horse trot around the ring. Vigor looked to be enjoying himself, but Alfie looked exhausted.

I followed him back to Vigor's stall, and leaned against the open doorframe. Alfie picked up a pitchfork and tossed manure into a wheelbarrow.

"This takes a lot of dedication," I said.

"What does?"

"All this shoveling, brushing and care."

He shrugged and said, "I enjoy being with the horses, and tending to them is part of it. Besides, doing my chores eases my mind."

His remark surprised me, and reminded me of Adena's. grandfather's comment. He was talking about meditation, which isn't always sitting in closed eyed contemplation. There's a myriad of ways to meditate, including tinkering on things, petting a dog, brushing a horse, or sewing quilts.

Alfie spread fresh bedding on the floor, then I followed him back down the hall. I stood at the gate as he entered the arena and called to Vigor. The horse trotted up to him and Alfie led him back to his stall. The wrangler went through the motions as if on autopilot, but he couldn't quite conceal his inner turmoil.

"I appreciate your thinking of me and stopping by," he said as he latched Vigor's door. "It's been a shock. I hope they find whoever did this to her."

Not waiting on my reply, he walked past me and out of the barn. Was that his way of saying goodbye? It was late and as much as I wanted to get on the road and home to Jake, I sensed it wasn't time to leave yet. I followed Alfie outside and took a seat next to him on a bench.

He pulled a pack of gum from his pocket, popped a piece in his mouth and offered me a stick.

"No, thanks," I said. We sat in silence, gazing at the stars. What should I say?

"The guilt's the worse part," he said.

"What on Earth do you have to feel guilty about?" I said.

"If I hadn't taken Faith to that pond, she'd be safe now."

"How do you figure that?"

"Because they must have seen us there."

"Oh? Did you ever see anyone there when you were with her?"

"No," he said.

"Then you don't know that to be true."

"But why else would they take her there?"

What could I say to ease his guilt? "One way to look at it is, in a different location her whereabouts could still be unknown. It might have taken years, if she was ever found. In the grand scheme of things, it was your special place and the horse she liked to ride there, that helped her get found."

He looked surprised. "That's interesting you'd say that. I was going to saddle Vigor for you to ride earlier, but he's had problems with his feet, so I chose Star."

"It's likely no coincidence I rode Star," I said. "There's a morsel of wisdom or deeper understanding in most things."

"So you think Faith would have come to harm, regardless of my bringing her to that pond?"

I nodded and said, "Yes, and as painful as this was, finding her offers closure. So why torture yourself with the unknown?"

He shrugged.

"Did you ever see the version of *The Time Machine* movie starring Guy Pearce?"

"Yeah, years ago, why?"

"Do you remember why Pearce's character tried to get that machine to work? Do you remember what his motivation was?"

"Sure, he wanted to explore time."

"Yes, but the reason was to save his sweetheart who had died. He worked for years to make the machine, successfully travels back in time, and prevents her murder. But something else happens to her. Do you remember?"

"Yeah, what about it?"

"For me, that scene exemplified how, even when he altered events, it was still her time to pass."

He looked at me. "Are you implying it was Faith's time to go?"

CHAPTER EIGHTEEN

"I BELIEVE WE go when it's our time to go," I said. "Just recently I astral traveled with a woman making her transition. But I couldn't follow her into the light. It wasn't my time."

He frowned, shook his head, then said, "But why would Faith choose to leave now? We had so many plans. And why in such a violent way? I should have protected her."

He was spiraling in guilt. I silently asked for guidance, and heard and repeated, "You are not the Keeper of the Universe."

He looked startled. "What does that mean?"

"It wasn't about you, or for you to control, so let go of the guilt. You mustn't blame yourself. And Faith could not have transitioned if it wasn't her time. But I sympathize with your distress. Someone dear to me died who I thought was too young. I was very distressed. Then I got a message."

"What was it?"

"It was a word, *enigma*."

"What does that mean?"

"Enigma means *paradox* or *corundum*. The message meant that his death wasn't for me to figure out. And it wasn't until I let go of trying to, that I was able to grieve."

He nodded. "I miss her so bad, it hurts," he said, rubbing his chest.

"Life holds many mysteries, and we may never fully understand them all, at least while still in the flesh. But while Faith's lifetime on Earth has completed, her spirit lives on."

"You really believe that?" he asked.

"Yes, I do," I said as she materialized next to him. "Her spirit, her essence is still very much alive."

He shrugged. "So if I let go of wondering why this happened, I get to grieve? Doesn't sound better to me."

"But you can then get to gratitude."

"Gratitude? What do I have to be grateful about?"

"You can be grateful for the time you had with her."

Tears spilled from his eyes and he dried them with his sleeve.

"Remember, enigma. If you're meant to know why, you will, but stop blaming yourself. Instead, each day find at least one memory of her in which you are grateful. It could be her personality, or something you experienced with her, or something she said. And it can be the simplest thing."

He nodded and said, "Faith had the most beautiful smile."

"She still does."

"What do you mean?"

"She's smiling at you right now."

He looked around. "Faith's here?"

"Yes, and she says she loves you and she's okay."

He blushed and said, "Thought I felt her around a time or two, but tossed it up to my mind playing tricks."

"When you sense Faith near you, don't dismiss it. She's just saying hello."

He nodded, and stood up, looking back at the barn. "All during that ride back here tonight, I debated about something, and I've decided to do it."

"What is it?"

"I'm going to adopt Bella's Star. She's a connection to Faith."

Faith smiled.

"Faith thinks that's a great idea!" I said.

"Thanks for stopping by, Jennie. Talking to you has helped me not hurt so much."

"Glad to be of service," I said. I stood up and handed him a business card. "If you ever need to talk, don't hesitate to call me."

He pocketed the card and said, "And if you ever want to ride Star again, be sure to stop in."

"Will do," I said.

"Well, thanks again. I have a few things to tend to before I head home," he said and walked back into the barn.

Curious, I followed him. He opened the door to a stall next to Vigor's, and stepped inside. I tiptoed up to the door and took a peek.

He spoke so softly to the horse that I couldn't hear his words. But Faith stood with him as he petted the muzzle of the beautiful black filly with the star on her shoulder.

☼

As I headed toward the Georgia state line, I burst into tears. I slowed the Toyota to a crawl and pulled off to the side of the road. During the entire ordeal I had suppressed my emotions. Now alone and on my own, I was overcome.

My Gifts serve to help the bereaved know that their loved ones live. But I had failed to be of such service to Paula.

"It's not your job that people accept the messages," Mica said.

"Thanks, Mica, but did Paula hear my message?"

The Serenity Poem that I had memorized as a child came to mind, and I recited it. "God grant me the serenity to accept the things I cannot change..." I couldn't change the outcome of what happened to Faith, but I hoped I brought closure. "Courage to change the things I can..." Had I tried my best to deliver messages to Paula and Mathias? Their anger had frightened me. "And the wisdom to know the difference." Had I made a difference? Had I helped anyone? I think I helped Alfie.

And while I understood Paula's frustration and rage, it was sad to think she believed God was vengeful or capricious. While I had no idea if Faith's grand plan included getting murdered, her soul knew. At our spiritual core we are wise, loving and eternal beings.

I said a prayer of peace for Faith, Alfie, Paula and even for Mathias. After all these years of feeling jilted by Mathias, I was now glad we stopped dating back in school. The man scared me, and I was grateful to be married to Jake. An image of my husband flashed in my mind, and I felt a tug of eagerness to get back to him.

It was past midnight by the time I resumed my drive. I switched on the radio, all I had to do was stay awake a few more hours.

☼

My heart leapt with joy when I turned onto the country lane that led to our cabin. It was three in the morning, so I was surprised when Jake stepped outside to greet me. He waited as I parked TLC, and in my haste to get to him I struggled to unfasten my seatbelt.

Once free, I ran to him, eager for his embrace. His scent was intoxicating, and he felt so comforting, I melted into him. We kissed and hugged and kissed again.

"I'm getting the impression you missed me," he said.

"A little," I said.

He laughed as we walked inside. I stood in the foyer, taking in the view. Jake had set a vase of fresh cut flowers in the living room, and the cabin looked wonderfully homey and inviting.

Taking my hand, Jake led me upstairs to our bedroom. I was exhausted as we got ready for bed.

Thankfully, while Jake was full of questions he said it could all wait till tomorrow.

We climbed into bed, and as I laid on my side he hugged me to him. I fell asleep, comforted by his embrace, and grateful to be home.

CHAPTER NINETEEN

THE NEXT MORNING, I rolled over to hug Jake, but he wasn't in the bed. I heard a skill saw and ran to the window. He was on the dock, setting a board in place. And he looked irresistible in his flannel shirt and jeans.

I quickly showered and dressed, then ran downstairs, outside and down the path. "Good morning," I said over the loud ping of his hammer.

He looked up at me from where he knelt and dropped the hammer to the deck. He stood up and removed his goggles as I stepped onto the floating platform. "Morning," he said.

The dock swayed as I walked up to him, pouting. "I woke up alone."

"I was letting you sleep."

I smiled. "Thanks, I do feel rested." His hair and clothes were covered with sawdust but he had such a woodsy scent I had to hug him, and did.

"You're getting dirty," he said as he brushed flecks of sawdust from my hair and sweatshirt.

"I don't care," I said, then paced the dock with my hands behind my back, as if inspecting his handiwork.

"You approve?" he asked.

"Yes, I do. It looks like you didn't need your Dad's supervision after all."

"Well, once I got started it just seemed to come together. It'll be nice to have the new decking when the kids are here this summer."

Our family reunion was at Jake's thoughtful invitation. I looked forward to my children and grandchildren all being here and the buzz of activity they will create. I cherished the rare times we were all united; a rare treat considering our geographic separation.

"And speaking of summer," Jake said, "I bought two Jet-skis at the marina yesterday."

"You did? Where are they?"

"At the marina. We'll get them when we take the boat out of storage. I also ordered a floating platform to moor them."

"You were a busy guy. I wasn't gone *that* long."

"I knew what I wanted to get, so it was just a quick phone call to the marina. Didn't take much time, and I'm sure Kate and Nathan will enjoy them."

"That's thoughtful of you," I said, grateful that he loved my family and that they loved him. And the grandkids were calling him, Papa.

"And I bought something else while you were gone," he said. "It was delivered yesterday."

"Oh? What is it?"

"I'll show you after lunch. It's in the garage."

I looked toward the garage and said, "Is it a pony?"

He shook his head and laughed. "Why on Earth would you think that?"

I shrugged.

"No, it's not a pony, but it does have horsepower."

"Is it a Ferrari?"

He laughed again. "No, it's not a Ferrari or a pony, but it's fun to ride."

"Well, I can't imagine what it is."

"No? But I thought you were psychic."

"Guess I'm too hungry to get a signal. Have you had breakfast?"

"I ate earlier, but I'll be ready for lunch in about an hour."

"I'll just eat something to tide me over," I said, then kissed him.

"You're making it more difficult to focus on my chores," he said as he pulled the goggles over his eyes. He knelt on the dock and picked up his hammer.

As I walked up the path to the cabin, the pinging sound from his driving the nails echoed in the cove. I'm sure the neighbors will be relieved when he's done making all that racket.

I went into the kitchen and ate a granola bar, then carried a mug of hot tea to the living room. I pulled my cell phone from my pocket and phoned Deanna.

"Hi, Jennie, what's up?" she asked.

I updated her about Faith, telling her all that had transpired since we last spoke.

"It's amazing the horse took you to the pond to discover her body," she said. "The odds of finding her were surely stacked against you."

"Oh? I'm glad you didn't tell me that before."

"Well, that's why I prefer working cold cases. I don't like the pressure of having to find someone when minutes count. But like with Faith helping you, much of my success has come from the deceased's assistance."

"Much, but not all?"

"Yes, unfortunately in some cases the deceased doesn't help."

"Why is that?"

"Some spirits have no interest in their past life. As for others, it's an enigma."

There's that word again. "If I had known the odds were so against me, I doubt I would have had the confidence to follow the clues."

"Yes, well ignorance is bliss as they say."

"Well, I'm glad it's over. And I don't want to get any further involved."

"Why not?"

"I don't want to go to court."

"Oh, no need to worry about that. The police and FBI aren't likely to officially recognize psychic help. And I doubt Wick will publicly acknowledge you. If he does, your contribution will likely be attributed to acute observation, good luck, guessing or reasoning skills. Besides, to my knowledge psychic clues aren't admissible in court."

☼

After talking to Deanna, I opened my laptop and typed in my journal. I had a lot of catching up to do, and was so absorbed that Jake startled me when he stepped in the room.

"Are you finished with the dock?" I said.

"Yes, finally," he said.

"That was quite an accomplishment."

He smiled and said, "Yes, I guess it was. I'm gonna take a quick shower, then we can eat lunch."

"Take your time," I said, "I'll be right here."

Jake walked upstairs, and I returned to my journal. But I couldn't focus. All I could think about was him, standing naked in the shower, his body covered with frothy bubbles.

I set the computer aside, dashed up the stairs and stripped on my way to the bathroom.

He looked surprised... then delighted when I stepped into the shower.

CHAPTER TWENTY

THE DAY WENT by quickly as we tended to some overdue housekeeping. Our spring cleaning included reorganizing the closets, rearranging some furniture, and hanging framed photos of the children. The cabin now felt more like ours than his, and I enjoyed tending to our nest.

Feeling dusty and sweaty after all our work, Jake first, then I took quick showers. After dressing, I found him downstairs in the living room. He had started a fire and had placed a chilled bottle of wine, two wine glasses and a platter of sliced cheese and apples on the coffee table.

"Thank you," I said as he poured the wine. He handed me one of the glasses, and we carried them over to the front windows.

"We might get snow tomorrow," he said, pointing north. We could see the higher peaks in North Carolina turning white with new snowfall.

My shoulders sagged.

"What's wrong?" he asked.

"I wonder how Paula, Mathias and Alfie are doing."

He hugged me and said, "What you need is some fun."

"What do you have in mind?"

"That thing in the garage."

"What's in there?"

"You'll know soon enough," he said with a smile.

"You sound so mysterious," I said, as we sat on the sofa and nibbled the fruit and cheese.

"I guess I do. Now I have to tell you something," he said, suddenly serious.

"What is it?"

"I don't like that you took such a risk going alone to North Carolina. I need to know you are safe."

I nodded and said, "Don't worry, I plan to work only from my office from now on."

He smiled. "That's good to hear," he said, and refilled our glasses. "So tell me about your trip."

I omitted the hard rain during my drive there, or that Mathias and I had dated, or that he came on to me. Instead I told him about their lovely house, their dog named Duke, their large vegetable garden and tree lined property, Faith's artistic talents and Paula's quilt room.

"We could make space for a sewing room if you want one," he said.

"What, no vegetable garden?"

He laughed and said, "Maybe when we retire."

I nodded, then described Faith's bedroom, the photograph of Faith and Alfie, and the beautiful sunflower quilt. Then I told him about my lucid dreams.

"So who's Reno, Mitch and Juliet?" he said.

"They're in my spirit group."

"Am I in your group?"

"I wouldn't be surprised," I said, then told him about the hag transforming into a lovely actress.

"Fascinating how she shape shifted like that," he said.

"Yes, it's similar to what spirit communicators do during my readings. A spirit can mirror the different stages of his life, depending on when he last knew the sitter. The actress appears as a hag to Mitch because it's how he remembers her."

"Can you help Mitch get over his fear?"

"That's a good question, and something I intend to try if we meet again."

"You mean you might not meet again?"

"I'm not sure," I said, and took a sip of wine. I told him about Bella's Star appearing in my dream, and how she's the same horse I rode from the ranch.

"I don't like that you rode horses with two strange men," he said.

"Stop worrying. I didn't sense I was in danger; and I'm home safe with you now."

He nodded. "So where did you go on the horse?"

"Star took us to the pond where we discovered Faith's body." I told him about driving to the ranch on my way home last night, and I repeated my conversation with Alfie. "He's adopting Star, and I hope Wick gives him Faith's locket."

I shared with Jake all I had clairvoyantly seen involving the crime; the man who hit her and the driver of the red car, how they hid her body in the pond, and the red paint on the boulders. "When I told the detective about the man slapping Faith so hard it broke her neck, he looked surprised," I said.

"So you told the detective everything?" Jake said.

"Yes, and I assured him that neither man was Alfie."

"But you don't know why they took Faith, or what they argued about?"

"No, not yet," I said. I told him how Wick drove me back to Paula's house, that I waited outside with Duke, and how shocked I was by Paula's anger. "I wasn't prepared for it. I just wish I had given her comfort. But she was too upset to hear me," I said. "I feel I've failed her."

"In what way?"

"The purpose of mediumship is to uplift and help the bereaved, and prove the continuity of life. I didn't give any of that to Paula."

"Why assume that? You told her Faith was okay, and you found her daughter's body. Why do you presume you didn't help her?"

"Because," I said, my words catching in my throat, "of the way she told me to leave."

"Well, she was overcome with loss, but that doesn't mean you didn't help her."

I nodded. "It's so hard to lose our loved ones. Do you still miss Connie?"

He stiffened at the mention of his first wife's name.

Why had I asked that? Was I that insecure?

"I miss Connie at times," he said. "But my feelings for her have nothing to do with my love for you."

"I understand," I said and sipped my wine, wishing we could change the subject.

"I once heard a theory," he said. "That we're born with various exit points. Kind of like a cat with nine lives."

"That is interesting. So a near fatal incident could have been an option to leave?"

"Something like that, And if so, I've had more than a few already."

"Oh? Like what?"

CHAPTER TWENTY-ONE

"WELL, WHEN I was young, I got a severe shock while plugging a cord into an electrical outlet. I didn't realize that my hand was touching the prongs," he said. "It was so painful as the electricity circulated my body with a painful *bang* of release at my bare feet, then *bang* up to my head, and another *bang* back to my feet again. It seemed like an eternity till the energy dissipated, but it was probably minutes before it abated."

"That must have been painful," I said.

"It was. But at least one good thing came out of it," he said with a mischievous smile.

"What was that?"

"It gave me my electrifying personality!" We laughed, then he said, "How about you? Any near misses?"

"Yes, and two involved water," I said. "The first incident happened when I was a toddler. I had wandered away from my mother while she was outside hanging clothes on the line. Unbeknownst to her, I toddled down the grassy hill, onto our dock, and fell into the lake. I don't remember any of that, she told me the details years later.

"But what I clearly do remember was bobbing in the water while a discarnate voice told me that help was on the way. I don't know if it was a guide, an angel or a spirit, but the presence comforted me and must have kept me from drowning."

"I wonder how long you were in there," he said.

"I have no idea, but it was at least several minutes. The second incident occurred when I was seven years old. I was swimming in the ocean when a succession of large waves knocked me underwater. Every time I tried to break the surface another wave pushed me under and over. I was a strong swimmer, but was running out of breath as I tumbled along the bottom. I began to panic, when a voice told me to push hard off the bottom. As soon as I was able to get some footing, I gave a hard shove. Once free, I swam as fast as I could to shore with the waves crashing over me the whole way. Thankfully, the crests grew shorter as I neared the beach, and I climbed onto the sand exhausted."

"That must have been frightening, especially to a child."

"Yes, it scared the heck out of me, and took quite a bit of coaxing by my mother before I'd dive back in."

"All this makes me wonder if our passing's predetermined."

"An astrologer once told me that both the time of our birth and death are significant. She said we are born and die right on time."

"If that's the case, close calls must not be our time to go," Jake said.

"Yes, and I'm glad it wasn't my time yet, or I wouldn't have become a mother, or a grandmother, or opened my store."

"Or become my wife."

"Yes, that, too. I guess what happens to us affects others more than we realize," I said, and ate a piece of cheese.

"I just had a thought. Maybe our soul doesn't measure a lifetime by age or years, but by accomplishments."

"That's an interesting way of looking at it. But even a hundred years is only a blip along an eternal timeline," I said, and chewed a slice of apple.

"We've been talking about death, but think what a miracle life is," he said. "I read that the odds of being born are astronomical. But is it random, like winning a lottery?"

"I think our soul plans its birth parents, body, time and place, so it must have some influence on which sperm fertilizes the egg. As for those who say we choose to be born for some achievement, the soul must feel confident that it can accomplish that despite any challenges or adversities we might face. And some might choose more difficult challenges in a lifetime."

"That's interesting," he said. We ate the remaining cheese and apple slices, then Jake said, "So we come to the Earth, experience stuff, then turn back into spirits."

"Not quite, we are always spiritual beings. And only a portion of our spirit comes into the body. Liken it to an astronaut in a spaceship. His ship contains databanks and computers for logging his journey. If he decides to get some specimen or make a repair, he leaves the spaceship wearing his spacesuit. The spacesuit helps him function in that atmosphere. But when he returns to the ship he no longer needs to wear the spacesuit or its tether.

"Likewise, a portion of our spirit is tethered to our higher self while in the human body. When our Earth journey is over, our spirit leaves the physical body and the tether, or silver cord, snaps as we reunite with our higher self. And like the logs in the spaceship, the higher self has memory of all our incarnations."

"That's a good analogy," he said, "you should use it in one of your workshops."

"Yes, I'll make a note of it."

Jake stood to stretch, and said, "One thing for sure, we might as well enjoy our time while on Earth."

I agreed. We looked out the windows and saw that the sun had set. Another day over. Jake closed the curtains, then said, "What do you want to talk about now?"

I set my glass on the table, and said, "Come here and I'll tell you."

He walked up to me. "What?"

"I've missed you."

He sat next to me and we kissed, lightly at first, then with deeper affection. I was hungry for him, and helped him remove my blouse.

He kissed my neck and shoulders as he unhooked my bra. I groaned with anticipation. We stood up to remove our clothes and I admired his form. I sat on the sofa and pulled him to me, taking my time pleasuring him.

He groaned, then took my hand and led me to the rug in front of the fireplace. We enjoyed and explored each other, and I quivered with release as we climaxed.

He held me close, and said, "Welcome home."

"I'll have to leave more often."

"No, I don't think so."

We sat with our backs against the sofa, and I wrapped a quilt around us. He put his arm around me while we gazed at the fire.

My stomach growled. "Do I smell lasagna, or am I just hungry?"

"There's lasagna in the oven," he said.

"When did you make dinner?"

"While you were in the shower."

"Did I take that long?"

He laughed and said, "No, it was already made. I just popped it in the oven. But I did make the salad."

We dressed, and I followed him to the kitchen. When he opened the oven door the aroma of baked lasagna filled the room.

We enjoyed a delicious meal, and for dessert we repeated my welcome home.

CHAPTER TWENTY-TWO

THE FOLLOWING MORNING, we decided to eat breakfast on the porch. But it was a bit cool, so we wore our jackets. We only had a few more days before heading back to Florida, and I was reluctant to leave our mountain getaway. But I've not yet been here in summer, so I looked forward to returning here for my first swim in the lake.

"Are you ready for your surprise?" Jake asked, interrupting my thoughts.

"You mean the one in the garage?"

He nodded and grinned.

"I can't imagine what it could be, but I'm grateful it's not a pony," I said rubbing my thighs. "I'm still saddle sore from riding the horses with Mathias and Alfie."

Jake's grin turned into visible anger.

"What's wrong?"

"I'm still not happy that you were alone in the woods with two strange men, especially when one of them could have been a killer."

"I never sensed I was in danger. Besides, I was there to help my friend."

"A friend you haven't seen in years!"

"So? What are you saying? Would you rather I sit in the house watching television all day? Would that make you happy?"

He walked away from the table and leaned against the banister, staring at the lake.

His remarks and behavior surprised me. I had no idea he was harboring such thoughts and feelings. And why bring it up now? The past is over and done. Why ruin what's left of our vacation? "You knew I was a medium when you met me."

He turned around, and said, "Yes, but I assumed you'd work out of your store."

"So did I! And I plan to work from there from now on," I said, no longer wondering what it'd be like to work free from an office. I had learned my lesson, and hoped my spirit guides were listening.

I carried our plates indoors, rinsed them, and loaded them into the dishwasher. I walked back outside, and found him still standing at the railing. I hugged his back, and said, "Let's not waste our time arguing. Can't you just let it go?"

He turned around and said, "I'm afraid for you. I never thought your job would put you at risk. But if you stayed indoors watching TV all day, you might be safe, but you wouldn't be who you were born to be. I guess I need to have more faith in your instincts."

"Yes, you do." My heart melted as we kissed. It's no wonder I kept falling more in love with this man.

He took my hand, and said, "Come on, it's time for your surprise." We walked up to the garage, and he said, "Close your eyes." He opened the door and led me inside. "Okay, open your eyes."

An orange four-wheel vehicle sat in the middle of the garage. "What is that?"

"That is an ATV."

"What's an ATV?"

"An all-terrane-vehicle."

"Oh? Where do you ride it?"

"On the OHV trails."

"And what are they?"

"Off-highway-vehicle trails, also known as ORV or off-road-vehicle trails."

Good grief; ATV, OHV, ORV? "When do we get to ride?"

"Well, there's a chance of snow today, so we'll set out tomorrow after breakfast. And we can grill lunch along the trail."

I climbed onto the seat and grabbed the handlebars. "Sounds like fun, but I'll drive."

"We'll see."

"So what will we do today?"

"I've got an idea," he said.

☼

Jake loved surprises. As he drove north, I asked, "Are we going to North Carolina?"

"No," he said, and pulled off the highway at a plant nursery.

I looked at the acres of plants, trees and ornamentals, and said, "Are we shopping?"

He nodded. "Yeah, thought we could spruce the place up."

Jake parked the Jeep and as I stepped out I nearly tripped over a yellow Labrador. "Hello, there," I said as I patted his head. "Are you the owner?"

"He thinks he is," said a woman who had followed the dog up the hill to greet us. She was slim and trim, dressed in jeans, a sweater and a denim jacket. She wore her long white hair braided with a yellow ribbon. And she absentmindedly pushed her wire rimmed glasses snug against her pretty blue eyes as she spoke. She removed her work gloves, and shook our hands as she introduced herself. "I'm Suzanne, and that's Rocky. How can I help you?"

Suzanne was attractive, and I was grateful when my husband acted like he hadn't noticed. "We need a variety plants for our yard and around the outside of the house," he said.

"Do you know what plants you want?"

"No, not really," Jake said.

"Well, the Georgia Blue makes a decent ground cover," she said as she led him down the steep gravel path into the nursery.

"Are there any plants you want, Jennie?" Jake asked as he stopped to look back at me.

"Yes, I'd like geraniums," I said as I petted Rocky.

Jake stared at me. "Aren't you coming?"

"I'll be right there," I said, as I knelt by the dog. I felt drawn to him, and I sensed he wanted to tell me something. "What's up?"

He blinked at me with sad eyes and his nose twitched.

I focused on his energetic field, and my stomach did a queasy flip. "Your tummy upset, Rocky?"

He whined as goosebumps flushed on my skin, a sign of speaking the truth.

"Jen, come on," Jake called to me from the bottom of the hill.

I ignored him as I kept my focus on the dog, and asked, "What is bothering Rocky's stomach?"

An image of a dog food bag flashed before my eyes. "Is it his kibble?"

"Yes," Mica said.

The dog blinked at me.

"Okay, Rocky," I said, "let's go tell Suzanne."

The dog led me down the gravel path, past hot houses and lean-tos, koi ponds and rock gardens. We found Jake and Suzanne in one of the greenhouses, discussing plants.

"Where have you been?" Jake asked.

"I was talking to Rocky."

Jake looked at the dog, and flinched.

"Can I ask you about Rocky?" I asked Suzanne.

She was reading the tag on a potted tree, and glanced at me. "What? What about him?"

"What are you feeding him?"

She looked confused, and stepped away from the tree, nudging her glasses against her face. "Why would you ask me that?"

"Because his stomach's upset."

"It is?" she said, looking at Rocky, then back at me. "How would you know that?"

"He told me," I said.

"My dog spoke to you?" she asked, looking from me to Jake, who shrugged and smiled.

"Well, he didn't actually talk to me," I said, "but he showed me."

She frowned. "What did he show you?" she asked the crazy lady.

Jake said, "My wife is a professional medium."

"You talk to dead people?" she said.

"Yes, and I guess dogs, too," I said with a smile.

She shrugged. "Okay, I'll play along. What's up with Rocky?"

"I sensed that his stomach was upset, and I saw a bag of dog food."

"Where did you see it? Did you go in my office?"

"No, it was a vision."

"I see," she said, crossing her arms across her chest, thinking. "Well, we did switch brands the other day."

"I'm sensing the kibble isn't agreeing with him. There's some ingredient in it that he's having trouble digesting."

She knelt next to her dog and said, "Is that true, Rocky?"

His belly rumbled so loud, one didn't need to be psychic to recognize his distress.

"Sounds like you do have a belly ache," she said, then looked at me as she stood up. "After we're done here, I'll go back to the store and get his other brand."

Rocky wagged his tail, walked over to a sunny spot, laid down and nibbled some grass. I hoped for his sake, she'd follow through.

"Can we get back to buying our plants now?" Jake asked.

I held his hand as Suzanne finished our tour of the nursery. She was so knowledgeable that we bought nearly every thing she suggested, along with a small utility trailer to get it all home.

☼

During the ride back to the cabin, I gazed at the potted geraniums on the back seat. I liked having the plant wherever I lived for it reminded me of one summer day many years ago, when my father and I planted geraniums as we sang songs.

Jake smiled at me, and said, "Can't take you anywhere."

"What do you mean?"

"I don't think Suzanne knew what to make of you."

"I guess."

"And I didn't know you talked to animals," Jake said.

"Well, if everything is connected in spirit or a unified field, why wouldn't we be able to communicate with the animals? I just hope Suzanne gets Rocky his other food," I said.

CHAPTER TWENTY-THREE

JAKE AND I spent the afternoon planting our new shrubs, plants and flowers. I found the task gratifying, and enjoyed getting my hands in the soil. My final chore was hanging the potted geraniums with the new hooks we installed on the back porch.

Jake toted the garden tools and empty pots to the shed, and I was reeling in the hoses when I heard, "Hi, neighbor."

I turned around and saw Margot watching us from her porch. She and her husband, Stan, had been friends with Jake's parents, and now kept an eye on the place for us when we're in Florida.

I removed my gardening gloves as I walked toward her yard, and shaded my eyes from the sun as I looked up at her. "Hi, Margot."

"You've been busy," she said as she pointed at our yard. "The new plants look lovely."

"Thanks," I said as I glanced back at them. "The lady at the nursery assured us they were hardy, so I hope they last till we come back this summer."

"Well, Stan and I can water them for you."

"You don't mind?"

"Not at all, we have to water ours anyway. Which nursery did you get them from?"

"Red Mountain."

"Oh, that's where we always go. Suzanne's been there for years and is very knowledgeable. I'm sure she gave you good advice."

"I hope so," I said as Jake joined us.

"Hi, Margot," he said.

"Hi, Jake. I was just telling Jennie that your plants are lovely."

"Thanks. I think they look pretty good."

"Yes, and Suzanne is very knowledgeable. She won't steer you wrong."

"That's what I've heard," he said, then nodded at me with that silent communication couples tend to do.

"Would you and Stan like to join us for dinner?" I asked.

"We'd be delighted," she said, "what can we bring?"

"Just yourselves," I said, noticing how quickly she had agreed to come.

"What time?" she asked.

"How about six?" I said.

"Great, we'll look forward to it," she said, then walked back inside her house.

"She must have been hoping for an invitation," I said to Jake.

"Why do you say that?"

"Because of her rapid response."

"Well, they do a lot for us."

"I know. I don't mind, but what will we cook?"

"I'm sure whatever you decide will be delicious."

"It's all on me?"

"Why? Don't you like to cook?"

"Yes, but..."

"So what's the problem?"

"No problem."

He hugged me. "Just kidding, I'll help."

"You will?"

"Yeah, I'll set the table," he said with a laugh.

"Gee, thanks."

"Hey, it's the least I can do."

"It certainly is."

☼

I ran up to the bedroom, closed the door, then stripped and tossed my clothes into the hamper. I stepped into the shower and was grateful we weren't on a well system so I could enjoy a long steam.

While lathering I noticed stubble on my legs, and lifted the razor from its holder. I balanced my right foot on the tile wall as I shaved, but the soap and the foam made the floor quite slippery. I lost my footing and, as if in slow motion, started falling face first into the tile shelf. I feared it would knock me out, or worse, as I fought to gain my balance. And then, for no perceivable reason, I shifted to the side and slammed into the wall. I was frightened, but not hurt. What's with me and water? I'm glad it wasn't my time to check out... again.

"What on Earth are you doing in there?" Jake asked as I turned off the water and opened the shower door.

He handed me a towel as I stepped on the rug, and said, "Guess I had another near miss."

"Oh? Are you okay?"

It was too embarrassing to talk about, so I simply nodded as he stepped into the shower. It was getting late, so I quickly dressed, then rushed downstairs to start dinner.

☼

Stan and Margot arrived promptly at six, carrying an apple pie and a bottle of wine.

"You didn't have to bring anything," I said as I took the items from them, "but thank you."

Stan and Jake went to the living room, and Margot followed me to the kitchen.

"How are Bobby and Brent?" I asked her, referring to their grandsons.

"They are doing well, and have adjusted nicely to being big brothers to the twins," she said.

"Darryl and Rita had twins? Isn't that wonderful."

Margot peered at me. "You can't fool me, Jennie. You knew they were having twins, didn't you."

"What do you mean?" I asked as I carried the pot of boiled potatoes to the sink and drained off the water.

"Last Thanksgiving when you and Jake ate lunch with all of us, was when Rita announced her pregnancy. But you seemed to assume she was carrying more than one baby. How did you know that? Are you psychic?"

I felt her eyes boring into my back as I mashed the potatoes. Margot was waiting for an answer. "I'm a medium."

She looked astonished. "Really? Are you serious?"

"Yes," I said as I carried the bowl of potatoes to the dining room.

Margot shadowed me as I walked back and forth from the kitchen, setting items on the table. "I've never met a medium before," she said. "Do you talk to ghosts? Can you see them?"

"Yes, I can."

"Do you do it for a living?"

"Yes, at my Sunflower Shoppe in Florida. I opened my store last September, and it's where I met Jake."

"Are you kidding? Jake went to a psychic? Why was he there?"

"To get a message."

"Really? Did he get one?"

"Yes, from Connie. And I have given him messages from his father."

"You have talked to Reginald?"

"Yes, the first time was when we were here last fall. He warned Jake about squirrels nesting in the attic."

"You mean you've seen ghosts here, too? Not just at your store?"

"That's right."

"Are there any here now?"

"Not at the moment," I said, and handed her a knife. "Would you slice the bread?"

She looked disappointed as she sliced the bread and placed it in the basket.

I called Jake and Stan to the dining room while Margot carried the basket to the table. We took our seats and Jake filled the wine glasses. As we ate, we all enjoyed friendly conversation, except for Margot who sat brooding.

About halfway through the meal, Stan looked at his wife and said, "What's wrong, Margot? You haven't said a word."

"Oh, it's nothing," she said, then glanced my way. Was she expecting me to give her a message?

After dinner, we all cleared the table, then Jake carried a tray of coffee cups and pie plates to the living room.

We sat in front of the fireplace, enjoying the coffee and pie, when Margot said, "Jennie told me the most amazing thing, Stan."

"Oh? What was that?" he said.

"She said she's a medium!"

Jake nearly spit out his coffee.

"She's a what?" Stan said.

"A medium," she said. "Isn't that fascinating?"

Stan looked at me as if seeing me for the first time. "Is that so?"

I shrugged, then nodded.

"So Jennie," Margot said as she set her cup on the table, "are there ghosts here with us now?"

I felt a bit put on the spot, but asked, "Do you mind, Jake?"

"Of course not," he said.

Margot rubbed her hands. "Oh, wonderful! This'll be fun."

I set my plate and cup on the table, closed my eyes and connected with the spiritual realms. When I opened my eyes I saw Jake's father's spirit, and said, "Reginald is here."

"Really?" Margot said. "Where is he?"
"He's seated on the arm of the sofa, next to Stan."

CHAPTER TWENTY-FOUR

STAN LOOKED UNEASY as he set his pie plate on the table.

"Reginald wants to thank you both for being such great neighbors," I said.

"Oh, isn't that nice," Margot said.

Stan shrugged, and sipped his coffee without comment.

"He thanks you for helping keep an eye on the cabin for us. And he congratulates you on your new grandchildren."

"Isn't that something, Stan?" Margot said.

"I guess so," he said.

"You guess so?" she said, "Why aren't you more enthused?"

"Well, no offense Jennie," he said as he set his cup on the table, "but anyone could have said all that. And I've heard about how psychics draw information out of you and study your body language, so they never divulge anything out of the ordinary. And while I wouldn't go so far as to call our neighbor a fraud, Jennie knows we were friends with Reginald. And she knows about our new grandchildren."

"But last Thanksgiving, Jennie knew Rita was carrying twins," Margot said.

"Is that so?" he said.

I nodded.

"Could've been a lucky guess," he said.

"Stan, really, where are your manners? I'm sorry my husband's so rude, Jennie," she said.

"Now, see here, Stan…" Jake said.

"Please everyone, stay calm," I said. "Stan's entitled to his opinion."

"See?" Stan said picking up his coffee cup, "No harm done."

"No, no harm at all," I said. "And from what I'm hearing, you always were opinionated."

Stan looked surprise. "Why would you say that?"

"That's what he told me," I said pointing toward the window.

Everyone looked at the window, then back at me. "Who's he?" Stan asked as he set the cup on the table.

"He's a spirit who's happy for this opportunity to say hello to you. His name began with an A," I said as my hand swept an imaginary alphabet, "followed by another A, then an R… His name was Aaron."

That got Stan's attention. "Aaron you say?"

"Yes, and he's wearing a military uniform and says he was in the Service with you. He's showing me something," I said as I held open my palm and studied an image there. "It's a lovely silver photo frame," I said, "but there's no picture in it."

'What does the frame mean?' I silently asked the spirit communicator. "He says that he gave this frame to you for your lady friend. No, that's not right," I said as Aaron shook his head. "This was a gift he bought for his fiancé, but *you* gave it to her. He says, 'Thank you for giving the frame to Dee."

Stan looked stunned. "I gave that frame to his Delilah when I returned to the States."

"Because Aaron never made it back. Isn't that right?" I said.

"How could you know that?" he said.

"I don't, but Aaron does."

Stan looked from Margot, who also looked stunned, to Jake, who was smiling. "Which one of you told Jennie about the frame Aaron bought Dee?"

"I didn't tell her," Margot said shaking her head.

"I never heard about it, so how could I?" Jake said.

"You must have known; I told Reginald about it," Stan said.

"Well, Dad never told me," Jake said.

Margot looked at me and said, "What else does Aaron say?"

"He's gone now," I said, "but a little boy is standing next to your chair, Margot."

"He is?" she said.

"Yes, he's about one years old and is wearing a vibrant blue sweater. He's walking over to you now, Stan, and touches your chin. Now he's back by Margot, and leaning against her leg. He hasn't given me his name, yet; maybe he's shy," I said, and asked the spirit for more information.

I opened my palm to see if he'd place anything there, and he did. "He is showing me a toy teddy bear, and it's now wearing his blue sweater."

Margot gasped.

Stan jumped to his feet and said, "Now, see here. Stop this right now! Can't you see you're upsetting my wife?"

"Sit down, Stan," Margot said, "let Jennie talk. I want to hear this."

Stan took a seat, but he was visibly angry. For some reason, I had touched a nerve.

"The child tells me that he was your son," I said. "He wants you to know he's okay, and he is with Pops and Noni."

"That's my parents," Margot said. "And the child you are talking about was our son, Adam. So he knows who we are?"

"Of course. He says he visits you often, and knows about Darryl. He wants you to say hello to his brother for him."

Tears fell to Margot's cheeks. Jake ran to get tissues, and returned handing her a box. "Thank you," she said.

Stan jumped from his seat and paced. "I need a drink!" he said.

"But don't you see, Stan? We never told anyone about Adam, so how could Jennie know?" Margot said. "Do you still doubt her Gifts?"

Stan sat down, but didn't reply.

Margot looked at me and said, "I got pregnant soon after we married. Adam would have been our first child, but he was stillborn. I had knitted a blue sweater for him, and put it on the toy bear Stan had bought for him. We dressed Adam in a little suit and placed the bear in the casket with him. But we've never talked about it, it was too painful."

Stan dabbed his eyes with a napkin, then said, "Looks like I owe you an apology, Jennie."

"That's quite all right," I said.

"No, it's not! I was rude and arrogant, especially as a guest in your home. I apologize," he said, "but I never wanted anything to do with the occult."

"Apology accepted. And the word *occult* just means *obscure* or *hidden*," I said.

"Well, that may be true, but I've always worried Margot would get taken in by scam artists."

"It's wise to be cautious," Jake said, "but there are legitimate clairvoyants."

"If you seek a medium, find one who gives evidence," I said.

"What do you mean?" Margot said.

"I'm referring to evidential mediumship. It's when the medium gives information about the spirit that the recipient can acknowledge. An example of evidence was the blue sweater on the bear, the soldier's name and the silver picture frame."

"Well, if I ever need a medium, I'll call you," Margot said.

Stan nodded and said, "This has been insightful."

"I'm happy to be of service," I said.

Jake smiled and said, "Isn't Jennie amazing?"

"Yes, she is," Margot said.

"Spirit's amazing, I'm just the instrument," I said. "I give all credit and thanks to the spiritual realms."

"Still want that drink?" Jake said.

"No," Stan said as he and Margot stood to leave. "It's getting late, and my wife and I need to finally talk about our son."

"Yes, it's time we acknowledge Adam, and tell Darryl he had a brother. Thanks for everything," Margot said.

We escorted them to the door. Stan stopped and turned to face me. "Don't ever let a bully know-it-all like me keep you from doing what you do," he said.

"Thank you, Stan," I said.

"I mean it," he said, "you have a real Gift."

We said good night and when Jake closed the door, he said, "That was fun."

"I'm glad it turned out well."

"Yes, and as much as I've seen you work, it still amazes me."

"Spirit still amazes me, too," I said.

Jake nodded. "And now it's time to share with you what's been on my mind all evening."

"Oh, what is it?"

"It's that vision of you stepping out of the shower earlier. I haven't been able to get it out of my mind."

"But that was hours ago."

"Yeah, I know. Tell me about it," he said as we walked up to our bedroom.

CHAPTER TWENTY-FIVE

JAKE WOKE ME, and said, "Are you ready for your big adventure?" As I opened my eyes he was standing by the bed, leaning over me, and already dressed. "Your breakfast is on the table, lunch is in the cooler, and the ATV trailer's connected to the Jeep. Let's go have some fun!"

"ATV?" I mumbled, foggy from sleep. Oh, yeah, the all terrain vehicle.

"I'll see you downstairs, Jake said as I rolled out of bed.

I nodded, then shuffled into the bathroom, feeling stiff and sore from all the planting we did yesterday. Between that and riding Bella's Star, I've used muscles I haven't used in years.

I took a quick shower, toweled off and dried my hair, then I went to my closet, and debated what to wear. How warm would it get? How cool was it now? I better dress in layers. I pulled on a tank-top, a T-shirt, a flannel shirt, jeans, and two pairs of socks. I grabbed my cellphone, then gingerly stepped down the stairs wearing my thick soled hiking boots.

Jake sat sipping his coffee, waiting for me. As I sat at the table I saw that he had made my favorite breakfast.

"You made French toast? Thanks!"

He smiled and said, "You're welcome."

French toast became one of my comfort foods during a family vacation when I was young. For that entire week, for reasons I can't now recall, Dad and I ate breakfast alone together at the hotel restaurant. And each day we both ordered the French toast.

Because it was so rare to have time alone with him, two of my happiest childhood memories are always triggered at the sight of French toast, and geraniums.

As I carried our empty dishes to the dishwasher, Jake said, "Bring along your windbreaker, I've already packed our winter coats and gloves in the Jeep."

"How cold do you expect it to get?"

"The forecast calls for only a slight chance of snow. But don't worry, we'll be fine. Ready to go?"

"I guess." I'm so used to the heat and humidity in Florida, that any dip in temperature can get too cold for comfort. I ran to the bathroom one last time, then grabbed my windbreaker, purse and keys as I headed outside. After locking the front door I walked up to the utility trailer. I've never ridden an ATV on an ORV before, so I wasn't sure what to expect.

"There's plenty of room on the trailer for another ATV should you become passionate about riding today," Jake said with a wink.

☼

He drove out of town, then turned north on Route 64. We rode nearly twenty minutes before he exited onto a gravel road that climbed in elevation.

"Where are we going?" I said.

"A friend of mine has property up ahead that adjoins the National Forest. We'll park and ride from there."

"You've ridden from here before?"

"Yes, he and I used to ride ATVs and dirt bikes here years ago," he said, then patted my leg and smiled. "You look so apprehensive. Don't worry, it'll be fun."

But I felt a sense of foreboding as Jake turned onto a dirt road that led to a field. He crossed the pasture and parked parallel to the fence at the far side of the property. "The trail is through those woods," he said, pointing past the fence.

I stowed my purse under the seat, and said, "I don't suppose there's a bathroom around here."

He laughed. "Only the ones Mother Nature provides."

"I hope it doesn't come to that."

"Try not to think about it," Jake said as we got out of the Jeep.

He opened the tailgate and jumped on the ATV. It roared to life as he started it. He backed it off the trailer and brought it around to the side of the Jeep. He strapped the cooler, a rucksack and our heavy coats onto the carrier. "Ready for your adventure?"

"Ready as I'll ever be," I said with a nervous flip in my stomach. I straddled the seat behind him and hugged his back, wrapping my arms around his waist. This was a perk I hadn't anticipated, and I cuddled into him.

We rode out of the pasture, through the woods and onto the trail. As he drove, I enjoyed the cool breeze and the warmth of the sunlight filtering through the trees. I relaxed my grip and sat back to gaze up at the brilliant blue sky, grateful to be outdoors.

As we climbed in elevation, the bare trees on our left offered a panoramic view of the valley below. We were up high enough for the houses to look like small toys. I caught sight of several farms, a snaking river and a distant lake. Come summer, the leaves will block these long range views.

The roar of the ATV echoed along the embankment on our right, making it futile to look for wildlife. But it felt good to be in the forest, and I enjoyed inhaling the crisp mountain air.

We rode for nearly an hour before Jake cut the engine. "How do you like it so far?" he asked as we stood to stretch our legs.

"It's wonderful. I'm loving the fresh air, the woods and the view."

"There's another trail with better scenery, but it's a rocky and rough ride."

"I'd rather not get bounced around all day," I said.

"Are you hungry?"

"Yes, but I can wait."

"No reason to wait," Jake said and carried the cooler to a clearing. He opened the lid and handed me one of the two wrapped foil packages. "I hope you like hotdogs," he said.

"I thought we were going to cook."

"Disappointed?"

"Not if this was easier for you," I said as I unwrapped the foil.

He nodded. "Thought this would be quicker as there's several places I want to show you today."

I bit into the bun. "Why does food taste better outdoors?"

"Yeah, I know," he said, then swatted at something.

"What was that?"

"Looked like a yellow jacket!"

"It might be attracted to the mustard," I said. "Years ago, my uncle was stung in the mouth when he bit into a hotdog."

"That must have been awful. But I heard they're attracted to sweet foods, so it was likely after the relish." He took another bite, then smacked his cheek. "Ouch!"

"What's wrong?"

"Damn thing stung me! Let's get out of here," he said as he tossed the rest of his bun away from us. "That should keep him busy," he said as the yellow jacket flew toward the bread.

Jake grabbed the cooler, and we ran back to the ATV. After he secured the cooler on the rack I grabbed some ice and pressed it against his cheek.

"Just hop on. I got something for the sting, but first let's get away from here."

I tossed the ice cube and jumped on the seat. He started the engine and sped several yards up the hill, then parked.

He hopped off, rummaged through the rucksack and took out a tube of ointment. "This stuff works great," he said as he dabbed the cream on his cheek.

"Are you going to be okay? Shouldn't we head back?"

"No, this will ease the pain and swelling. Besides I want to show you something." He jumped back on the four-wheeler, but now as he drove, I was no longer watching the scenery. Instead, I was looking over his shoulder trying to learn how to drive this thing. If he got dizzy or ill from that sting, I'd need to get us back to the Jeep. That is, if I could find my way back to the field.

We rode around a bend and Jake braked so hard I slammed into his back. I looked past his shoulder and saw a black bear up ahead on the trail. It stood on its hind legs and must have been six feet tall. We must have startled the bear as well, for he waved his paws at us.

"Don't look him in the eye," Jake said as he put the ATV in neutral and slowly backed down the trail.

I looked away, frozen with fear to my seat.

Finally, the bear dropped to all fours and ran into the woods.

"Holy crap," I said, "I nearly peed my pants!"

CHAPTER TWENTY-SIX

"I THOUGHT I smelled a bear," Jake said. "Good thing I was paying attention or we would have run into him."

"You smelled him? What do bears smell like?"

"They have a musky scent, kind of like urine. Unless that was you I was smelling," he said with a laugh.

"Very funny!" I said, playfully slapping his back. "But I thought the bears would be hibernating this time of year."

"The males emerge about now, but the females with cubs stay in their dens longer."

"So there could be more bears out here?" I asked as I peered at the deep woods.

"It's possible, you never know what you'll find when you're out in nature."

"Well, so far we've found yellow jackets and a bear. Maybe we should head back."

"Not yet," he said and drove higher up the mountain.

In another twenty minutes, he pulled off and cut the engine. "Come with me," he said, taking my hand. He led me through the woods to an outcropping. "I've seen eagles up here."

We walked up close to the edge, and looked out at the expansive view of the distant mountains, lakes, rivers and the valley below. And the birds soared, not just above, but below us. It was paradise!

We sat on a boulder, quietly contemplating and meditating. It was a wonderful experience, and I was grateful Jake had brought me here.

☼

"I've got one more place to show you before we head back."

He drove a mile or so down the other side of the mountain, then veered off the trail and into thick woods. We came upon a stream that flowed across our narrow path.

"Lift your feet to keep your boots dry," he said as he drove through the shallow water and parked on the opposite bank. We got off the ATV and he pulled what looked like two cake pans from his pack.

"What are those?" I said.

He knelt by the stream, and dipped one of the pans into the water then swirled it around. "These are mining pans. You fill the pan from the stream, then shake and swirl it around. If there's any gold it'll be the heaviest thing in the pan and will sink to the bottom." He slowly rinsed away the layers of sand by adding more water. "Once all the sediments gone, the ridges in the pan will catch the gold."

I knelt beside him as he handed me a pan. We filled them from the stream and started sifting.

"Did you know that twenty years before the 1849 California gold rush, the first US gold rush happened near here in Dahlonega, Georgia?" he said.

"No, I didn't know that."

"Yeah, and Dahlonega gold is said to be purer than the standard. And the phrase, 'There's gold in them there hills!' was referring to Dahlonega."

"I had no idea," I said.

"We'll have to go to the Dahlonega Gold Museum so you can watch their historic film about the prospectors and the mining."

After swirling several panfuls of water, I said, "Well, there may have been gold in them there hills then, but there's none here today."

"We'll try another spot," he said. As we walked back toward the ATV, he stopped and pointed at a fallen tree. "See how that tree's hollow at the end? That's the type of spot rattlesnakes like to hide." He walked closer to it and said, "You just have to be careful to... uh-oh!"

"What's wrong?"

"There's a huge snake on top of that log and he's looking at me!"

"Get away from him!"

Jake took a step back and stopped. "Oh, shit!"

"What now?"

"Look at the ground!"

I looked closer and noticed that the brown leafy forest floor was moving. There were snakes all around where Jake stood. "Jake, get out of there!" I said as I jumped onto the seat of the ATV.

"I'm trying," he said, as he backed away, slowly lifting one foot then the other.

The big rattler slithered from the top of the log and into the hollow opening where Jake said a snake would like to be. The noise from all the rattlers sent chills through me as Jake took a giant leap toward the ATV.

"Ouch! Oh, shit!" he yelled.

"What is it? Did a snake bite you?" I asked, my heart pounding.

"No, but something stung the back of my hand. I think it was a hornet. Holy shit that hurts!"

I jumped off the ATV and searched the sack for the ointment. Finding the tube, I handed it to him, then shoved the wet pans into the rucksack. "Can you drive?" I asked as he rubbed salve on his swelling hand.

"Yes," he said. "Hop on!"

Jake sped across the stream with no concern for our boots getting wet. He raced up the hill, flew past the panoramic lookout and sped down the mountain.

I was in dire need of a pit stop but not willing to pee around bears, yellow jackets, hornets or snakes. I willed my bladder to hold on, which was a miraculous feat considering the bumpy ride.

☼

At last, Jake took a sharp left and drove us onto the open field. It was a most welcomed sight.

"I need a restroom ASAP!" I said.

"Use the woods," he said.

"I don't think so."

"If you can wait, there's a few restaurants not far from here," he said, and winced in pain as he set the ATV on the trailer.

"What's wrong?"

"Can't you see my hands swollen? It hurts like hell!"

"Hey, it's not my fault!"

"Sorry to snap at you, Jen, but you'll have to unload the gear."

"We need to get you to a hospital," I said as I placed the cooler, rucksack, coats and hats in the Jeep.

"No, I'll just soak my hand when we get home."

"Then let's head home now."

"No, I'll put more ointment on it. Besides, it won't take that long to eat, and you need to pee," he said as we raised and locked the tailgate together.

"Do you want me to drive?"

"No, get in," he said. We slid onto the front seats, and Jake said, "What's your pleasure? There's Chinese, Mexican, Italian, Barbecue or Greek."

"Whichever has the nearest bathroom," I said, gritting my teeth and crossing my legs.

☼

Jake pulled into a shopping center and stopped at the curb. I leapt out and ran to the nearest restaurant. I waddled to the bathroom, thankful to find the facilities clean and unoccupied.

I walked back to the dining area and found my husband seated at a table with two glasses of wine. I sat next to him and took a sip.

"This'll warm us up after that brisk ride," I said.

"Were you cold? Why didn't you say something? I would have stopped for your coat."

"I didn't want to stop, besides you shielded me from the wind. But weren't you cold?"

"No, I guess all that adrenaline kept me warm."

"I'm glad that ride's over."

"What? You didn't enjoy our adventure?"

I laughed. "It's something I'll remember for a long time."

"See that? Wasps, bears and snakes make for a memorable trip."

"It's the view at that outcrop and looking down at the soaring birds that I prefer to remember."

"Yes, that's always been one of my favorite spots."

"I can see why, and I did enjoy our outing. But I was worried during our ride back to the Jeep."

"Worried about what?"

"That I'd have to drive."

"Now that would be scary!"

"Hey! Very funny! I'm a good driver. I just never drove an ATV."

We placed our orders, and while we waited for our food to arrive, I admired the ornate Chinese décor. A distant memory popped into my mind. It was again from my childhood, and I was dining with my father at a Chinese restaurant in New York City.

It was amazing to uncover a third memory where I was alone with him. I don't remember why or what brought us into the city, but I'll tuck that memory in with the geraniums and the French toast.

Each memory was precious in that it was rare to spend quality time alone with him. And those moments were unique, because most of the time he was aloof and indifferent, much like Ben. Is that familiarity what initially attracted me to my first husband?

I looked at Jake and he smiled at me. I was thankful he was not like Ben or my father. Jake was always kind, thoughtful, loving and attentive, and with him I didn't need to savor rare memories, for every day was a good day.

CHAPTER TWENTY-SEVEN

AFTER DINNER I asked Jake if he wanted me to drive.

"Why?"

"So you can rest your hand," I said as we walked toward the Jeep.

He pointed at the trailer and said, "Have you ever towed anything?"

I shrugged. "No, but I have to learn sometime. It can't be that hard, and it's a pretty straight shot down the highway. Give me the keys," I said, extending my hand.

He hesitated, then said, "I hope I don't regret this" as he tossed me the keys.

I sprinted ahead to open the passenger door for him, then ran around and slid onto the driver's seat.

He gave me a few preliminary instructions, and said, "Remember, if you pass someone, that trailer's behind you. Be sure to use all the mirrors and be mindful of distance. You don't want to cut someone off when you come back into the lane."

"Don't worry, it'll be fine," I said. I put the key into the ignition, but my hand froze as I looked through the windshield. Two men were walking toward the sidewalk, and in seeing them, I felt a chill.

"That's them," Mica said.

"Ready to go?" Jake asked.

"No, look! Those are the men."

"What men?"

"The men who killed Faith."

"Are you sure?"

"Positive."

"How can you be so sure?"

"Because Mica is," I said as we watched them walk into the auto supply store. "I need to phone Wick." I pulled my cell along with the detective's business card from my purse, and dialed his number.

When he answered, I said, "Hi, this is Jennie Walker. Paula Mear's friend."

"Yes, what can I do for you, Ms. Walker?"

"I just saw the two men who killed Faith."

"You did? Where are they?"

"They're in an auto supply store here in Franklin."

"When did you see them?"

"A few minutes ago."

"Are you sure it's them?"

"Yes, I am."

"Are they in there now?"

"Yes," I said and gave him our location. "My husband and I are sitting in our Jeep at the outer edge of the parking lot. You can't miss us, we're towing a utility trailer."

"Whatever you do, don't make contact with those men," Wick said. "They could be dangerous. We'll be right there."

"What did he say?" Jake asked as I disconnected the call.

"He said he's coming," I said, feeling a rush of anticipation.

"Good, let's go home."

"What? We can't leave!"

"Why not?"

"Because I have to stay and point them out to Wick."

"No, you don't. You told me you gave Wick their sketches, so we don't need to be here."

"It'll be fine. I'll identify them and we'll leave."

"You think that's all there will be to it? You stay and identify them and you'll be facing them at their trial."

"No, I won't. Deanna said she doesn't go to court for cold cases."

"But this isn't a cold case."

He might have a point. I chewed my lower lip, then remembered something else Deanna said. "No, Jake, Deanna said that the clues we provide are not admissible in court."

"I don't know about that."

"Well, she does, so relax. I want to see this through. I owe it to Paula."

"You don't owe her anything, and I'd like to get home and soak my hand in Epsom salt."

"Oh, please, Jake. Let's wait on Wick, then we'll leave and I'll take care of you."

Jake scowled at me as we rolled down the windows, and waited in silence.

☼

Two patrol cars pulled into the parking lot. "Must be Wick's backup," I said.

Jake glanced at them, but didn't say anything. Minutes later, Wick's sedan pulled into the parking lot and drove up next to us. He rolled his window down, and said, "Evening, Ms. Walker."

"Good evening," I said, "this is my husband, Jake."

Jake nodded hello to the detective.

"Good evening, Mr. Walker," Wick said. "Are the men still in the store?"

"Yes, they are."

"Do you know which vehicle is theirs?"

"I hadn't thought of that," I said.

I silently asked Mica to make their vehicle stand out to me. I scanned the parking lot and noticed a shimmer. "It should be that red car over there."

He radioed to one of the patrol cars about the red car. Within minutes Wick received a reply.

"The tag comes back as a stolen a vehicle," Wick told us. "Can you describe them and how they're dressed?"

"Yes, one is tall and thin with long dark hair and a beard. He's wearing a tan jacket and a blue cap. The other man is shorter and stocky with short hair. He's wearing a green jacket, no hat or beard."

Wick relayed this information to the officers as we gazed at the store.

"Okay, you gave the description, let's go," Jake said.

"Wait," I said as the front door opened. The two men stepped onto the sidewalk. "There they are now!"

"Stay here," Wick said.

"We will," I said as Wick drove away.

"Let's go," Jake said.

"Move!" Mica said.

But I tuned them both out as I was too caught up in the drama.

"You've identified the men and their vehicle. Wick has your phone number if he has any questions. Let's go," Jake said.

"Please wait a little longer, Jake. Wick might need something."

Jake was about to reply when we heard a loud crack.

"What was that?" I asked.

"Sounded like gunfire! Drive away from here now!" Jake said.

But I couldn't react. I was mesmerized, unable to believe what was happening.

The two men were crouched behind a pickup truck, and the police were shielded by their cruisers with both sides shooting at each other. An officer got hit, and fell to the ground.

Mica said, "Duck!"

I ducked down against the steering wheel as something buzzed through the open window and the rear window exploded!

"That bullet hit the ATV. Get out! Run away from the Jeep!" Jake said.

"What?" I was too stunned to move. Jake unbuckled our seat belts, reached across my lap and opened the driver's door. With a forceful shove he pushed me out as another buzz flew past.

I landed on the asphalt with a hard thud that brought me to my senses. I jumped to my feet and ran for refuge at the far end of the sidewalk.

Jake joined me there, and was about to say something, when there was a blinding flash of light followed by a deafening explosion.

"What the heck was that?" I said. My ears were ringing as I looked to where the bright light had been and saw our ATV engulfed in flames!

The cashier from the Chinese restaurant peeked out the front door and asked, "What the heck is going on out there?" then ran back inside, not waiting for a reply.

I watched the police arrest the two men, then looked at Jake. He was holding his neck, with blood seeping through the swollen fingers of his hornet stung hand.

"Oh my God, were you shot?"

Jake glared at me.

The detective walked by and I yelled, "Wick help us!"

He ran up to us, and said, "What happened?"

"My husband's been shot!"

"It's just a graze," Jake said, wincing as Wick looked at his wound.

"Hang on, Mr. Walker, I'll get help."

"Oh, Jake, I'm so sorry," I said.

He didn't say anything, which frightened the heck out of me. "Are you mad at me?"

He didn't answer, and refused to even look at me. I felt a pang of panic, as it's the first time he's ever been aloof.

The ambulance pulled in and Wick waved them over to us. A firetruck drove in as well. They must have seen the firelight from miles away. While the firefighters soaked the ATV with foam, a paramedic cleaned and bandaged Jake's neck.

Why hadn't my spirit guides warned me that he could get shot? Had they tried to tell me, but I failed to receive the message? And if they had forewarned me, could I have prevented it?

"Lucky it's just a graze. Looks like you've had a rough day," the paramedic said as she also tended to Jake's swollen hand and cheek.

"You could say that," Jake said as he pointed at our Jeep and the charred remains of the ATV on the foam coated trailer.

"Do you need a ride home?" she asked him.

"No, he doesn't!" I said, and escorted Jake back to the sidewalk.

Wick walked over to check on us. "You okay, Mr. Walker?"

Jake nodded.

"I want to thank you for your help in apprehending those men, Mrs. Walker," Wick said.

"Glad I could help. But what caused that fiery explosion?"

"Bullets must have hit the ATV's gas tank, causing it to leak. One of our officers took advantage and created a diversion by tossing a lit flare into the gasoline puddle. That blast stunned those guys enough for us to nab them. Thankfully we succeeded before anyone else got shot. We got lucky."

"Yeah, lucky," Jake said.

"Is the officer that got shot okay?" I said.

"Yes, he was wearing a bulletproof vest," Wick said.

Wick walked away as a fireman approached us and said, "Is that your vehicle?"

"I'm afraid it is," Jake said.

"The Jeep looks okay other than the blown rear window and the paint peeling off the back. But I'm afraid the ATV's totaled. The trailer looks to be on its last legs. You could call a tow truck, but depending on how far you're going, it might make it there if you take it slow."

CHAPTER TWENTY-EIGHT

WITHOUT SAYING A word, Jake got to his feet and headed toward the Jeep. As I caught up with him he was walking around it, surveying the damage. He pulled open the driver's door and slid onto the seat. He was starting the Jeep as I opened the passenger door.

"Are you leaving me here?"

Without answering, he put the Jeep in gear and coasted forward as I buckled my seatbelt. After a few feet, he parked and jumped out to check the trailer. He got back in, adjusted the mirrors, and drove out onto the highway.

What's with the silent treatment? "Aren't you speaking to me?"

He ignored me as he drove, constantly checking his mirrors.

"Those guys are in a lot of trouble," I said. Jake made no reply. We drove several miles, and the silence became deafening. "Please say something."

He glared at me and said, "I'm too angry to talk to you, Jennifer!"

My stomach flipped. He never called me Jennifer; it was always Jennie or Jen. And I've never known him to be this angry. It's not that I feared him physically, but his emotional abandonment made me nauseous.

"I'm so sorry," I said, speaking rapidly. "I hadn't planned to see those men tonight. We picked that restaurant location at random. And I'm sorry the Jeep got damaged, and the ATV destroyed. And I'm very sorry you got hurt. But I'm grateful it was just a graze. Oh, please talk to me, Jake."

Silence.

☼

Jake backed the trailer off to the side of our garage, then jumped out and disconnected the hitch. He climbed back in the Jeep and drove it forward a few feet, then parked.

He pressed the remote, then walked in the garage, returning with the wet-vac. I got out and stood nearby as he vacuumed broken glass from the Jeep.

"Aren't we going to discuss it?" I said.

He put the vacuum away, closed the garage door and carried the rucksack and the cooler into the house. I followed him inside, carrying my purse and our coats.

I hung up our coats and my jacket, then went to the kitchen where I emptied, dried and stored the cooler in the pantry.

Jake grabbed a beer from the refrigerator, popped aspirin in his mouth and took a swig.

"Should you be drinking alcohol with those pills?" I said.

He walked out of the room, up to our bedroom and slammed the door. I waited a few moments, then followed him. When I entered the room, the bathroom door was closed and I could hear the shower running. I sat on the bed, waiting, and hoping he'd calm down.

I heard the water shut off and moments later he opened the bathroom door and stepped into the bedroom. He towel dried his hair with one hand, and sipped beer with the other. He glared at me as he tossed the towel on the bed and got dressed.

"Please, Jake, say something."

His anger startled me as he turned toward me, pointed his finger in my face, and said, "You put us in needless danger! I told you several times to get us out of there. But no, you just had to stay longer and put our lives at risk."

"But I didn't mean to..." I said.

"I don't want to hear your excuses! When you use your Gifts to help people communicate with their loved ones in spirit, that's a good thing," he said. "And finding Faith was helpful, I guess, though I'm still not happy that you drove into that violent storm, or that you rode horses with two strange men!"

How did he know I had driven through that storm? I purposefully left out that detail earlier. I started to say something, but he looked so angry I kept quiet.

"You wanted me to talk, so listen! Using your Gifts in your store is one thing, but not in the vicinity of armed murdering car thieves. You cannot put yourself or others at risk. What if Evan or Lola or Emily had been in that back seat? You even think of that?"

I shuddered at the idea of putting my grandchildren in danger. "But they weren't there!"

"No, they weren't, but we were, and we came damn close to getting killed!"

"I'm sorry..."

"Your saying sorry doesn't mean shit! I want you to say... no swear... that there will never be a next time!"

"But I had to help Wick. I owed it to Paula."

Jake tensed. "You owed that woman nothing. Now, because of your recklessness, I've been grazed by a bullet, the Jeep and trailer are damaged and the ATV destroyed. And because of that, I'll probably have to testify at their trial. Jeez, thanks a lot. Are you sorry about that, too?"

He grabbed the towel from the bed and carried it to the bathroom. He returned, took another swig of beer, and said, "You always say your Gifts are used for love. And that's great, I'm all for it. But acting like a superhero on some adrenaline high is not going to cut it. And I can't understand why your spirit guides would put us in such danger." He drank the last of the beer, and tossed the bottle into the waste basket. "By the way, why did you duck?"

I flinched. "What do you mean?"

"As the bullets whizzed by us, you ducked against the steering wheel. Why did you do that?"

"Mica."

"What about Mica?"

"Mica said to duck," I said.

"Would've been nice if you had warned me."

"It all happened so fast; there wasn't time," I said. "And you might have ducked into the path of a bullet. Maybe the warning wasn't for you, and not telling you saved your life."

He mulled that over, then said, "I'll give you that one as possible. And I'm glad to hear that Mica warned you. What else did Mica say?"

I shrugged.

"Mica didn't tell you to leave? Mica didn't try to get us out of danger before the bullets started flying? All Mica said was duck?"

I stared at the floor.

"That's what I thought. So you not only ignored me, but Mica too."

I nodded, and burst into tears as I realized the depth of my error. I looked up at him and saw blood seeping through the damp bandage on his neck. I wiped away my tears as I stood up, took his hand and led him to the bathroom.

I carefully removed the wet bandage from his neck, and nearly fainted when I saw his wound up close. He was right, this was my fault. And he would soon wear a scar as a constant reminder of my actions.

But even if he was mad at me, I was glad he was still here, grateful his soul hadn't decided to check out this day. I silently thanked God for protecting him as I dabbed ointment on his neck. My hands shook and tears filled my eyes, making it difficult to apply the fresh bandage. "I'm so sorry, Jake."

"Tell me what I want to hear," he said.

"You know, I'm not the only one who put us at risk today."

"That's true," he said, "but when I sensed danger, I moved us away from it."

"I didn't know those men would be there or have guns, and..."

Jake glared at me and said, "Wanna try again?"

"I'll try to be more careful."

"Close, but no cigar," he said.

"I promise to be more careful and not ignore Mica's warnings."

"I hope you mean it." His eyes softened, and he said, "I'll be downstairs."

After showering and dressing, I took a moment to question my guides. "Where had I veered off course and put us in harms way?'

"When you were impressed to leave, but didn't. But we're pleased you ducked. You are not asked to be unsafe," Mica said.

As much as I hated to admit it, I had ignored the warnings. I was too caught up in what was happening. And I'm glad that I'm not asked to be in danger.

I walked downstairs and found Jake sitting in the living room, staring into space,. As I sat next to him he said, "The oddest thing happened when that bullet grazed me."

"Oh? What was it?"

"My entire life flashed before my eyes. It was very fast, yet I saw everything from my birth till now. And it made me realize just how precious and fleeting life is."

CHAPTER TWENTY-NINE

THE NEXT DAY Jake had the Jeep's rear window repaired, but decided to have it repainted after we get back to Florida. We spent the rest of the day packing and readying the cabin before our drive home.

We headed out early the following morning. And I was glad that Jake was talking to me again, acting more like himself during the long ride home.

We exited off I-75 in Central Florida, and stopped for takeout on our way in. As Jake pulled into our garage, it felt good to be back in Del Vista. As reluctant as I had been to leave the mountains, I now looked forward to getting back to work.

And I had learned to be more careful in what I wished for. Before our trip, I had envied Deanna's working without the confines of an office as she helped solve cold cases. My North Carolina experience helped me realize that I'd rather sit at my desk and give readings to my clients.

☼

Monday morning we didn't need an alarm clock to wake us. We were both up early, and eager to get back to our routines. As I toweled off from my shower, Jake stood shaving at the bathroom sink. I watched as he carefully shaved around his wound. I feared that scar forming there would constantly remind him that I almost got him killed, so his laugh surprised me. "What's so funny?"

"I was thinking of all the ways I could respond to inquiries about my injury. But anything I make up is not as unbelievable as the truth!"

☼

I turned onto Main Street, drove past the town square, and was thrilled when my Sunflowers Shoppe came into view. Mine was the only vehicle there this early as I parked my Subaru. Since moving out of the back apartment, it was rare for me to arrive before Megan.

The wind chimes welcomed me home as I unlocked and opened the front door. Once inside, I walked around opening the blinds and turning on the lights and displays. I stopped at Megan's desk and glanced at the appointment book. She already had my week filled.

The front door opened, and Megan looked relieved to see me. "You gave me a scare! I didn't know if someone had broken in, or if I had forgotten to lock up."

"Sorry to frighten you. I was eager to get started," I said.

"Welcome back. How was your vacation?"

"It was interesting, and eventful."

"Oh? How so?" she asked as she walked behind the counter to stow her purse, then turned on her computer and the cash register.

"Well, our first day there Deanna called and asked me to drive up to North Carolina to help find someone's daughter. Turns out, I went to high school with the missing girl's parents."

"Oh? Did you find her?"

"We found her body."

"Oh, I'm sorry to hear that."

"Yes, it was very sad for my friends. After I returned to Georgia, Jake took me on a trail ride up the mountains on his new ATV. We drove up so high that, when we stopped at an outcropping, birds were soaring in the valley below us."

"That's amazing!"

"Yes, it was. Too bad the ATV got destroyed."

"What? How?"

"It got totaled in the explosion."

She stared at me. "What explosion? What happened?"

"The police blew it up during the arrest."

"You got arrested?"

"No, not us; the men who killed my friend's daughter."

"Sounds like you had a stressful vacation."

"Well, at least the ATV ride was fun, other than Jake getting stung, bit and grazed by a bullet."

"What? Is he okay?"

"He's healing," I said.

"Remind me to never vacation with you."

I nodded, then pointed at the appointment book and said, "Looks like you've been busy."

She smiled and said, "Yes, we received a lot of requests for readings and sales were brisk all week. In fact I need to place an inventory order today."

I looked around and realized that the shelves were unusually sparse. "Thank you, for all you do."

She shrugged and said, "It's not work when you love what you're doing."

I walked over to the coffee counter, brewed a mug of tea, and carried it down the hall to my office. When I tossed my purse on the desk the silver spoon fell out. I had forgotten all about that dreadful spoon. I held it and said, "Bend! Bend! Bend!" but nothing happened.

I placed the spoon on the desk and looked at the time. My first appointment wasn't due for an hour, and if I remembered correctly Kate had the day off, for teacher's planning or something. I hadn't spoken to her all week, so I phoned her.

"Hi Mom, how was your trip?" she said when she answered my call.

I told her about driving in the storm to North Carolina, seeing my old school friends, riding the horse, and finding Faith. The ATV ride, the views, panning for gold, yellow jackets, hornets, snakes, the bear and the explosion.

"Good grief," she said. "Is Jake okay?"

"He's mending."

"I'll think twice about taking a vacation with the two of you."

"I hope that doesn't mean you won't be going to the cabin with us this summer."

"No, I'm looking forward to that, and so are Evan and Lola."

"Me too, I love having us all together."

"Anything else new?" she said.

"You mean other than my vacation?" I said, and eyed the spoon. "I'm still trying to bend spoons."

"You still haven't? Guess you're no Uri Geller."

"Guess not."

"What's the point anyway?"

"To prove to my rational mind that everything is energy. Besides, I'd like to make a wind chime of them."

"Maybe subconsciously you don't want it to bend."

"You may be on to something. My parents raised me better than to bend one of their spoons."

"Then, see it more as creating art," she said, ever the teacher. "And it would make quite a conversation piece."

"You're right. I'll try thinking differently about it," I said as I spun the spoon on the desk.

"Just don't stress about it. And once you're proficient at bending silverware, you can make me a wind chime, too," Kate said.

"If you really want one, you best make your own," I said.

"Now, Mom, you're the one who taught me about belief and expectation."

"Yes, you're right. So what's new with Lola?"

"That girl's been invited to so many birthday parties, I can barely keep up with her schedule. And it's getting expensive buying all those gifts. When I host her party, every one of those kids better show up!"

"And how's Evan?"

"He's still in Karate, and really likes it. He's earned several stripes and is working toward his next belt."

"That's wonderful."

"Yes, but I'm not pushing him. I'll take him for as long as he wants to continue."

"Well, I hate to hang up, but I have an appointment due soon."

"Okay, but I'd like to ask you something."

"Oh? What is it?"

"Would Jake come over and fix my clothes washer?"

"Well, I'm not sure he can repair it, but I'm sure he'd look at it for you."

"I hate to put him on the spot."

"No, he'd be happy to help you. When should we come?"

"How about tomorrow after work? And I don't expect him to labor for free, so plan on staying for dinner."

"Okay, and I'll bring spoons."

"Oh? Well, I guess I can at least try to bend one."

"Don't worry, you can't be any worse at it than I am."

Megan appeared in my doorway as I disconnected the call. "Your appointment's here. Are you ready?"

"I'm more than ready."

CHAPTER THIRTY

THE COUPLE SEATED across from me looked to be in their late forties. The woman wore a colorful red scarf over her long dark hair. She was short and plump, with dark circles under her eyes. Was it from lack of sleep?

The man was taller than her, and looked distinguished with the specks of gray in his thick black hair. And he had a handsome face, but a bulging nose.

From his body language, it appeared that he didn't want to be here. He remained silent as the woman spoke to me with a thick accent in broken English. "I am Carmen and this my husband, Vincent. He not want to come. I hear good things of you, so I make appointment."

"It's a pleasure to meet you both," I said.

She smiled at me, then to him said, "See, Vincent? She nice lady."

Vincent said nothing as he stared at the table.

"He's not same since Carlos passed. He's sad all the time, this not normal. He cannot pass the, how you say, the grief. You understand, yes?" she said.

"Yes, I think so," I said.

"Good, you help us," she said.

"I'll help in any way I can, but please understand, it's spirit who gives the messages, I only deliver them."

She nodded and waved her hand at me, "Yes, yes, you do now."

Vincent glanced back at the door as if plotting his escape. Carmen noticed and spoke rapidly to him in, I'm guessing, Italian. He shrugged, looking at me with dark hooded eyes. Something was troubling him.

"Does he understand English?" I asked her.

"Yes, he speak perfect," she said.

"Are you ready to start, Vincent?" I asked him.

He shrugged his shoulders.

I closed my eyes and connected with the spiritual realms. When I opened my eyes, a spirit stood behind Vincent in my symbolic place for father.

"Vincent, is your father in spirit?"

He nodded.

"He passed recently."

Vincent nodded again.

"Your father is here with us."

Vincent looked surprised.

"You see Carlos?" Carmen asked me.

I nodded. "He's pointing at his nose, Vincent, and he says that you had a nose like his until you broke it." Then the spirit showed me a scene of two men fighting. "Did you break it while boxing?"

Vincent gasped. "How could you know that?" he asked, then looked at his wife. "Did you tell her about me?"

Carmen shook her head, "No, Vincent, I swear." She looked at me and said, "Tell him, Jennie."

I nodded, but kept my focus on Vincent's father. "You have a brother?"

"Yes," Vincent said.

"He wants you to tell him he's okay."

Vincent nodded.

"Your father is dressed in a suit with two pins on the lapel. One pin is red, white and blue, and looks like an American flag. The other is green, white and red. This has significance."

Vincent gasped. "Yes, we buried him in a new suit, and my brother pinned the American and Italian pins on it."

Vincent's father spoke to me, and I said, "He thanks you and your brother for the pins and the new suit."

Vincent nodded, then said, "But how can my father talk to you? He didn't speak English."

"He speaks to me telepathically, so there isn't a language barrier." Carlos brought forth a new scene, showing me a brick wall. I wasn't sure if it was literal or symbolic, so I said, "He's now standing next to a brick wall. Does this have meaning to you?"

"Yes," Vincent said, "he was a bricklayer."

Vincent's father sent me a block of thought, and I said, "He says he is sorry he wasn't a better provider."

"No, you are wrong," said Vincent. "He took good care of us!"

"Yes, Carlos was good man to his family," Carmen said.

The spirit showed me a new scene, and I said, "Your father is showing me cigarettes. He started smoking as a teenager and never kicked the habit." I felt pressure on my chest, and said, "Did he have trouble breathing at the end?" I sensed this had to do with his death.

They both nodded, and Vincent said, "He had emphysema."

And with that acknowledgment, the pressure eased off, and I took a deep breath. Then I heard a song playing, low at first, becoming louder. The song was *My Way*, and I said, "Your father was a Sinatra fan."

"Yes," Vincent said, "he told you that?"

"Listen to her, Vincent!" Carmen said.

'Why her apprehension? What's troubling her?'

"She thinks he's doubting you," Mica said.

On the contrary, I sensed he was elated. With all the evidence he was receiving, he appeared happy with his father's visit.

I heard whistling and said, "Your father liked to whistle. He was generally a happy man, but could be quick to anger."

"This is true," Carmen said, nodding.

"Your father wants to tell you something."

Vincent flinched and Carmen held his hand for moral support. What on Earth did they expect him to say?

"Your father says he hopes you are listening."

Vincent squirmed in his seat.

"Your father says he often acted like a tyrant. You were afraid of him."

Vincent winced.

"And he says he's sorry."

Vincent and Carmen both gasped.

"Your father says he always wanted to toughen you up, so you could face what life threw at you."

Vincent's eyes reddened.

"He says that he didn't understand you, but now he sees that you are not soft, but kind. Kind like your mother was, but not a push over. You are strong, but a caring person."

"I told you Carlos loved you," Carmen said to him, then to me, "but Vincent not believe me."

"Yes, your father is sorry that he was so hard on you. He asks that you let go of the past and move forward with your life. He says that you have much life ahead of you, much to accomplish. And he says, 'I love you and I am proud of you, Vincenzo."

Vincent looked shocked, and said, "That is how he pronounced my name!"

That was good confirmation, because that was how I heard it.

Vincent sat quietly, contemplating the message. Would he take it to heart, or continue to live with resentment? That was up to him, he had free will.

And Carlos had one more message, this time for his daughter-in-law. "Carlos is giving you a bouquet of roses, Carmen. He says he is very happy you are Vincent's wife."

"Oh, thank you," she said.

Vincent's father nodded at me, then disappeared.

"Your father's message has been delivered."

Vincent's face was more serene than when he first came in. He even smiled when he said, "I understand Papa better now. I never felt good enough, that I was a disappointment to him. Now I see why he was that way. It's time to get past this."

Carmen clapped her hands and let out a shriek of joy so loud it startled me. "My Vincent is happy now, yes?"

"Yes," he said, and hugged his wife.

☼

After escorting them to the front of the store, I returned to my office. Vincent had been afraid of hearing from his father, but I have found spirit to always be loving and wise. I believe it's because in spirit we are no longer clouded by human emotions, and can see a bigger picture.

Spirit communicators mostly want to tell loved ones they are okay. But it's not uncommon for them to want to make amends. By helping their loved one, all mutually benefit.

And Vincent's father gave his son what he needed most to hear; a message of love and healing.

CHAPTER THIRTY-ONE

I HAVE USED music as an energetic boost between readings, so I was dancing to Chumbawamba's *Tubthumping* song when Megan came to my door.

"Your next appointment's here."

"Okay," I said as I turned off the radio.

Megan returned with a new client named Leah. The young woman was petite, with short hair and glasses that framed her friendly eyes. But she moved stiffly as she walked to the reading table. She took a seat, and folded her hands in her lap, looking attentive and expectant.

"Thank you for coming in today," I said.

"It's nice to meet you. My friend JD told me about you."

"Please tell JD thank you," I said, making a note to send Joyce Dillon another gift card. She was one of my first clients, and I was grateful for all the referrals she sends my way.

Leah said, "I've never been to a medium before, so I'm not sure what to expect."

"First, I'll connect with the spiritual realms, and a spirit will come forth. He or she will offer details that, hopefully, you can acknowledge as their presence. Then

I'll give you their message. Any questions before we begin?"

She shook her head and said, "No."

As soon as I connected with spirit I heard an old nursery rhyme, *And the dish ran away with the spoon.* When I opened my eyes I saw a vision of a small white square. It grew larger, and was embroidered with that line of rhyme along with an image of a spoon and a plate.

The white square then morphed into an apron, and a woman appeared wearing it. She then walked behind Leah's chair, one step up in my symbolic place for grandmother.

She had short hair, and her eyeglasses dangled from a beaded chain around her neck. The spirit waited and smiled at me as I described her to Leah.

"I remember my grandmother having an apron like that," she said. "I miss you, Grandma."

Her grandmother nodded, then I repeated what she said. "She loved to cook and nothing pleased her more than serving a big meal to her family." A vision appeared, and I said, "She is showing me a long table with people seated all around it as she serves platters of food. She says, 'The bigger the feast the better'. Cooking for her family was her passion and her bliss."

The scene changed to the kitchen where a pot of bubbling and blooping red sauce sat on the stove. But instead of *sauce*, I heard the word *gravy*. Why was her grandmother saying gravy when it was clearly spaghetti sauce? Was this significant?

So I did as I was trained, to give what I get, and said, "She is showing me a pot on the stove that looks like red sauce, but she's calling it gravy."

"Oh, yes," Leah said, "she always referred to it as gravy."

The spirit nodded and smiled at Leah. And I realized that Leah had gotten more evidence from my mention of gravy than she would have had I only said red sauce. The spirit communicators always amaze me with their wisdom. And I was once again reminded to trust my reception.

The vision returned to the dining table, and I said, "She is again showing me the dining room. There are so many people seated at the long table, they are crammed together. The adults and children all talk animatedly as one of the men carries in a big pot from the kitchen. He places it at the head of the table for your grandmother, and everyone passes their bowls to her to fill. She is wearing her dish and spoon apron. And while her family eats, she walks around the table kissing the top of each child's head."

"Yes," Leah said, "that is what she'd do. My parents, my brother, me and my uncles, aunts and cousins would all eat dinner at her house every Sunday."

"Your grandmother says that cooking was not a chore, but a pleasure. It wasn't just a meal, it was a way to unite her family each week." I sensed her joy at feeding her brood.

The scene changed, and the table was silent, collecting dust. Cobwebs hung from the chandelier. "Since her passing, no one has kept her tradition?"

"No, we hardly ever get together now except for Christmas."

The scene shifted again, and Leah was cooking at a stove while her grandmother's spirit watched her. "Your grandmother says you have her recipe box."

Leah smiled and said, "Yes, and I recently cooked her sauce for my family."

"She is pleased." I had delivered the evidential, it was time to receive her message. "Your grandmother is saying that when she fed her family those meals, she was also feeding them her love. Her joy was immense when she was surrounded by her family."

"I hope she isn't asking me to cook for all my aunts, uncles and cousins," Leah said.

"No, she is saying that was her bliss, and she wants you to live yours." Her grandmother nodded at me and I said, "She asks, 'What is your passion?"

Leah thought about it a moment, then said, "I guess it's cooking, too. But I don't want to cook for all my relatives every weekend."

"No, that was your grandmother's passion. What are ways to express yours?"

"I've wondered about publishing a cookbook of her recipes. I could build a blog about her cooking, but isn't that a dumb idea? There's already so many blogs out there. What do you think?"

"Sounds like a great idea to me, why not give it a try?" I said.

Her grandmother faded away, and another spirit came forward. Leah's reading was not over. This was a male spirit.

"There's a male spirit here who says he was your doctor." I felt tension in my neck. "Are you afraid of moving your neck?"

"Yes, it's been stiff for years," Leah said.

I saw a vision of a child in bed. "You were injured as a child and ordered bed rest?"

"Yes," she said.

"You had a very bad fall from a great height. You fell off a retaining wall?"

"Yes, outside my uncle's house."

"And you overheard this doctor tell your parents that you mustn't move your neck, which scared you." I saw a thick gray mist around her neck. *'What's this about?'* I silently asked. And the spirit told me about her fear.

"When this doctor told your parents that you mustn't move your neck, he didn't mean never; it was just for a while," I said.

She looked surprised.

"He says that a therapist, perhaps one using hypnotherapy, might be able to help you."

"Really? Can you recommend someone?"

"No, you might want to ask your physician for a referral. But if you hear a name more than once, perhaps in conversation, that would be confirmation from your guides."

The spirit of her doctor nodded and faded.

"Your messages have been delivered," I said. "And when you publish your cookbook blog, please send me a link."

"I will, and thank you, Jennie. I'm glad JD recommended you. I'll be sure to pass out your business cards as well."

After Leah left my office I reflected on my confusion at *seeing* spaghetti sauce while *hearing* gravy. It proved once again that I have to trust and just give what I get. Holding back doesn't serve anyone.

And all this talk about red sauce had me craving spaghetti, so guess what I'm cooking for dinner tonight.

CHAPTER THIRTY-TWO

THE FOLLOWING MORNING, Jake was already dressed and ready to leave for work when I awoke.

"Why are you up so early?" I said.

"The golf tournament's today."

"Oh, I forgot."

"I need to get in and help supervise things," he said.

"Will you be working late?"

"I don't think so, why?"

"We're going to Kate's tonight."

"Oh, yes, you volunteered me to fix her washing machine."

"Are you upset? She's grateful, and she's making us dinner."

"I'm just teasing. I'm happy to help her. I just hope I can fix it. I called my friend, Tom, about it. He knows all about appliances."

"Oh? Is he going to Kate's, too?"

"Only if I can't fix it."

"Then I better tell her to set an extra plate at the dinner table."

"What? You have no confidence in me?"

"Well, I wasn't aware your skills included appliance repair."

"I'll have you know I'm a man of many talents. And if I didn't need to get to work now, I'd demonstrate a few."

"Gee, how romantic. Too bad I can't take you up on that offer."

"Go ahead and be sarcastic, but if not for the tournament, we'd be playing hooky."

"Well, you'd be playing with yourself because I have to get to work, too."

☼

I parked in front of the Sunflowers Shoppe, then walked up and peeked in the front window. The top of Megan's head was visible behind the front counter. She must be at her computer. She's developed a sixth sense for what the customers like, so I let her do the shopping.

When I pushed open the front door the wind chimes alerted Megan. She looked up at me, and said, "Good morning. I'm glad you're here."

"Why? What's up?" I asked as I walked to the coffee counter and brewed a cup of tea.

"I'd like to go over this inventory order with you," she said.

"Why do you need my help?" I asked as I carried the mug to the front counter.

"If I buy what's in my shopping cart I'll be over budget."

"It's only money," I said.

"I'm glad you can be so nonchalant about my spending your money," she said with an easy laugh. "But I've promised to stick to our budget, and I can't decide which things to buy."

"What kind of things?"

"Well, look at these Himalayan crystal lamps," she said as she pointed at an image on her screen. "These are the best prices I've found."

"So what's the problem?"

"If I order the lamps, I can't order this lapis heart shaped pendant. Isn't it beautiful?"

The necklace was lovely. "Go ahead and order the lamps and four necklaces," I said.

"Four? Why so many?"

"One for you, one for me and two for the store."

"Really? Oh thank you, Jennie!"

"You are most welcome."

As we spoke an elderly woman came up to the front door, and looked in at us. I opened the door for her and she stepped inside using her walker.

"Good morning," Megan said, "how can I help you?"

"I'm here for my reading," she said.

"Are you Mrs. Clark?" Megan said.

"Yes, I am."

"You're early, your reading isn't till ten," Megan said.

"Yes, but my niece dropped me off before her errands. I'll just wait over there," she said, pointing at the waiting area.

"Hi, Mrs. Clark. I'm, Jennie."

"Hello," she said.

"There's no need to wait, we can start now."

"Oh, that would be lovely."

"My office is down the hall," I said.

She glanced at the long hallway, then at me and said, "I guess I can make that."

I walked with her as she took one slow step after another. I never before realized how many steps there were till I viewed the distance from her perspective.

It felt a bit awkward walking this slow beside her, so I asked, "Did you find us okay?"

"No, I didn't, but my niece found you," she said with a smile. "She's very good at finding things on that phone of hers."

"Well, that's good," I said.

"Yes, she's very helpful. All my children live up north, so she's the only family I have here in Florida. She has a busy life of her own, but still finds time to help me get groceries, and go to the doctor. And everyday she checks in on me. I'd be lost without her."

"She sounds very thoughtful," I said, realizing how fortunate Mrs. Clark was to get such assistance. "Here we are," I said as I ushered her into my office.

She slowly lowered herself into one of the chairs.

"I'll put this over here for you," I said as I stowed her walker by the door.

"Thank you," she said.

As I sat across from her I said, "What brings you here today?"

"Well, there's something on my mind, and I hoped you could help."

"What is it?"

"My husband died many years ago. At the time, we were both in our fifties. I'm now eighty-two. So when I die, I'll be eighty-two or older. Since he was only in his fifties when he passed, why would he want to be with this old lady when she dies?" She teared up as she spoke, and I sensed her distress.

"Let me share something with you," I said. "When I see spirit, their age and appearance is how the client can acknowledge them. So someone who died in infancy would come forth as an infant, and usually be accompanied by an adult in spirit. But this doesn't mean the spirit is forever a baby. And if you last saw your friend in college, her spirit would appear much younger than in a reading for her spouse or child. The age is part of the evidence for the message."

She nodded and said, "That sounds logical."

"Yes, and I've been told a spirit can choose the age he or she liked best. So you and your husband could choose to be the same age, even though he passed before you."

She looked startled. "You mean I won't be this old lady after I die?"

"No, your spirit body is not restricted by your Earth body's age or condition. When my mother first appeared to me after her passing, she looked to be in her sixties, the age at her death. A few nights later, she appeared to me again. But this time she was in her thirties, looking as I remembered her from my childhood. And she told me that when she first passed from her body, she felt as youthful and energetic as a seven year old."

"Oh, that's wonderful! So there's no need to fear my husband's age difference?"

I nodded as a young man in spirit appeared next to her chair. He wore a tweed jacket and held a brown cap in his hands. I described him to her, and she said, "That's how Kenneth looked when we married!"

"He mentions Chesapeake."

"We honeymooned near the Chesapeake Bay," she said with a smile.

The spirit nodded, then aged before my eyes. I described him again to her, then said, "He says that you need not concern yourself with age. He says, 'Don't fret, my Pet, all will be okay."

"Oh, Kenneth always said that when I was worried about something. I had forgotten that."

"He says that he will greet you when your time comes, and he loves you very much."

"Oh, it's so wonderful to hear from him! Please ask him about Monroe, Pierce and Reggie."

He nodded at me. "He says he's with them. Were they siblings?"

"Reggie was my brother, and Monroe and Pierce were his. We were all very close, growing up together in the same small town. Now I'm the only one left here," she said with a reflective sigh, "last one at the party. I hope to see them soon."

"You will be with them, but there's still time to be with your family," I said.

She looked saddened by that. "Who needs more time when they never visit or call me?" she said. "They'll be glad when I'm gone and they won't have to be bothered about me. I'd just as soon leave now, while I'm still healthy enough to not be a bigger burden to my niece. She has enough to do without tending to me."

"You are not a burden to her," I said.

Mrs. Clark smiled. "Marlene and I have always been close. When all the children were young, she was the one who followed me around. And ever since she learned to drive, she's visited this old aunt. She's always been thoughtful toward me."

"You have a special bond with her, something that stems from a past lifetime."

"You think so?"

"Yes, I do."

Her eyes moistened. "I've never understood why she cares so much more about me than my own children do. They're probably wondering why it's taking me so long to die."

"Sometimes we feel closest to those not nearest in blood," I said.

She laughed, and said, "Isn't that the truth."

I nodded.

"Don't fret," Kenneth said, and I repeated his words to her.

"Thank you," she said, "you've eased this old lady's mind. It must be nice to be able to communicate with the spirits like that. Your life must be so easy."

I smiled, and said, "We all have our challenges. And we all get guidance, but don't always choose to listen or acknowledge it. As for your children, have you called them recently?"

"No, I guess I got resentful at always phoning them."

"Well, I don't sense animosity toward you. They are caught up in their lives, but it's not that they don't care about you."

She nodded as I brought her walker over to her.

"Remember, don't fret," I said.

She smiled as she pulled herself to her feet. "I'll have to remember that," she said. "And you've given me peace of mind that Kenneth won't shun me."

"No, he won't, don't fret about that at all."

We slowly walked back to the storefront. A young woman, seated in the waiting area, stood up as we approached.

"All done, Aunt Tara?" she said.

"Yes, Marlene, and let me introduce you to Jennie. And that lovely young woman over at the counter is Megan," Mrs. Clark said.

"Yes, I met Megan when I came in," Marlene said with a smile. "And it's nice to meet you, Jennie, I really like your store."

"It's nice to meet you too. And I give Megan most of the credit for our storefront."

"Well, I'll be back to buy a few things I've seen for gifts," she said to me, then to her aunt said, "Will you join us for lunch?"

"Oh, that would be lovely, but I don't want to be a bother."

"You're never a bother, Aunt Tara. Don't fret."

Mrs. Clark looked stunned by the comment. "What did you just say?"

"Don't fret?" Marlene asked.

Mrs. Clark smiled. "I do have to remember that," she said.

I watched from the window as Marlene helped her aunt cross the street and get in the car. I sensed they've had many lifetimes together. And I couldn't help but smile at Mrs. Clark's comment that my life was so easy. If she only knew! I'm here for the human experience too.

"Don't fret," Megan said.

"What did you say?" I said, and walked over to the counter.

"Don't fret, Jennie. I found a coupon code online and saved our budget when I placed the order."

CHAPTER THIRTY-THREE

LATER THAT AFTERNOON Megan carried a large parcel into my office. “This just came for you,” she said as she set it on my desk. “What do you think it is?”

“I don’t know,” I said, and stood to read the return address label. “It’s from Paula Mear.”

Faith materialized by my desk. “I had a little something to do with it,” she said.

“Aren’t you going to open it?” Megan asked.

I grabbed my scissors and carefully sliced the packing tape. Megan helped lift open the flaps, and we found a large plastic bag inside. I opened the bag and saw tissue paper.

“What is it?” Megan said.

“It’s a quilt,” I said, and opened it enough to see which one. “It’s the sunflower quilt!” I said, and fell to my seat.

Faith nodded and smiled.

“Look, there’s a note inside,” Megan said as she handed me an envelope.

I opened the card and read it.

“What does it say?” Megan asked.

“It says, ‘Thank you for your help. Thought you’d enjoy this. Love, Paula’. Here, Megan, help me spread this out,” I said as I stood up and handed her one end of the fabric.

As we unfolded it, we admired Paula's exquisite stitching and design. The quilt was more lovely than I remembered.

"This is so beautiful," Megan said, "did your friend make it?"

"Yes, this was Faith's quilt."

"You mean the daughter who..."

"Yes, it was on Faith's bed when I slept there. I'm amazed Paula would part with it. I'm so touched, I'm speechless."

"You need to call her," Megan said.

"Oh, I don't know about that. She practically threw me out of her house."

"How can you not call her after she sent you this?" Megan said as she helped me fold the quilt.

I set it on the sofa, and thanked her for her help. After she left the room I shut the door and Faith said, "Call Mom for me."

I sat on the sofa next to the quilt, rubbing its soft fabric with my hand as I placed the call. My stomach flipped when Paula answered. "Hi, Paula, it's Jennie."

"Did you get the quilt?"

"Yes, I just received it. But I'm surprised you'd send it to me."

"Least I could do."

"How are you doing?"

"About as good as can be expected."

"Taking it one day at a time?"

"Yeah, I guess. At least those guys confessed, so I won't have to sit through a trial. I'm grateful for that," she said.

"Yes, that is a blessing," I said.

"They claimed they only meant to scare her."

"Have they said why?"

"From what I was told, Faith had threatened to turn them in. She and a fellow student saw them selling drugs on campus. Faith told her advisor that she was going to tell the police. Turns out the advisor knew the men and warned them to stay off campus. The men told the advisor that they'd scare Faith into keeping quiet. And even though the advisor told them to leave her alone, she's in trouble now, too."

"So that's what they argued about?"

"Guess so, that's their story anyway. And the other student has come forward and told the police that she and Faith had planned to report the dealers. But when she heard about what happened to Faith she got scared."

"That's understandable," I said. "Have you seen Alfie?"

"Yes, he came by to show me Faith's locket. Detective Wick returned it to him, and he asked if I was okay with him keeping it. I told him he should have it; he bought it for her."

"I'm glad he got the locket back."

"Yeah, and did you know they were engaged?"

"Yes, he told me."

"We had no idea. They planned to tell us that weekend. He asked for some of Faith's things, but I told him I wasn't ready to sort through her belongings yet. But I did want to send you her quilt."

"I can't thank you enough."

"You're welcome," she said. "And I'm sorry for how rude I was to you. It wasn't your fault what happened."

"Don't fret," I said.

"Thanks, and I guess you heard about Mathias."

"No, how would I? What about him?"

"He's moved out."

"Oh, I'm sorry."

"You needn't be, it was my idea."

"Why? What happened?"

"The final straw broke. For years I've pretended I was in a blissful marriage for the sake of my girls. I wanted them to have a happy home, so I turned a blind eye to his drinking and cheating. But Faith's passing caused me to reevaluate things, and I decided that life's too short to live short-changed."

"Are you okay?"

"Yes, and it shouldn't come as a surprise to you, Jennie. Mathias always had a wandering eye. Did he hit on you while you were here?"

Had she known? I didn't want to admit he had.

"Your silence tells me he did," she said with a sigh. "And didn't you date him back in school?"

"Just for a while," I said.

"Well, I guess Mathias was famous for jumping from one girl to the next, but by the time a friend warned me about him, it was too late. When I told Mathias I was pregnant, I didn't expect him to step up, but he did, and swore he'd never cheat. But soon after we married, I learned he was. I tried to make a home for him, and after Faith's birth a few years later, I hoped he'd finally settle down. But he didn't. It was as if he couldn't help himself. His cheating ways turned me off, and it's been years since I've let him near me.

"After Faith passed away, his drinking, cheating and anger escalated. With Faith gone, and Joy living in New York, I no longer had a reason to keep up the charade. So I told him I wanted a divorce, and he left. It feels odd sometimes for him to not be here, but overall it feels like relief."

I silently asked Faith if her mother was ready to hear a message.

She nodded and said, "Tell Mom I didn't suffer. Tell her I'm okay."

"Paula, can I give you a message?"

"Sure, what is it?"

"Faith is showing me that she was surrounded by a vibrant white light of loving and peaceful energy when she passed. She didn't suffer, and she's okay. She says she was greeted by her grandparents. She comes near you often, so talk to her. She can hear you."

"I miss her so much," Paula said, the words catching in her throat. "How do I talk to her?"

"Just talk. And you can try to connect with her by journaling or meditation."

"I don't know how to meditate."

"There are numerous ways. Try just sitting quietly and focusing on your breath for fifteen minutes. In time, you will go longer and deeper. As for journaling, write about your thoughts, feelings and dreams. You can also write a letter to her."

"She was so young," she said.

"I know, but I believe that at the soul level we are aware of what we might experience before we're born. Faith is saying that she stood up to her bullies, and didn't back down as she had in previous incarnations."

"But it got her killed!"

"Maybe so, but try to understand that only her spirit knows why she passed when she did."

"I'm too angry to accept that, and I've stopped praying," she said.

What could I say to that?' "Meister Eckhart, the German theologian, mystic and philosopher, said, If the only prayer you say in your entire life is thank you, that will suffice."

"What do I have to be thankful about?"

"For the time you had with her. And I believe death is a doorway, so when it's your time you'll be with Faith again."

"Oh, I don't know. Will it ever get easier?"

"It'll take time to process your grief. But even though my mother passed away years ago, there are still days I wish we could meet for lunch. So no matter how much we study or learn about spirit, we can still miss the physical connection of those we hold dear."

"I know what you mean, I still miss my mother, too."

"Please be patient with yourself. You are dealing with a lot right now. Maybe you should see a therapist to help you through not only Faith's passing, but Joy's moving away and your divorce."

"Yes, maybe I should."

"And Faith's happy Alfie has her locket, but she'd like for him to also have her engagement ring."

"All right, I'll give it to him," she said.

"And Faith mentions your new lipstick."

"She knows about that? I bought a new shade of red lipstick yesterday at the grocery store. Silly, I guess. It was on a whim, but I felt like it cheered me up a bit."

"Well, according to color therapy, red boosts self esteem. And wearing any shade of new lipstick lifts my mood."

"Yes, and it's funny she'd mention the lipstick, as she was forever borrowing mine. I'll think of Faith when I wear it. Thanks, Jennie."

"You are welcome. And please call me anytime."

"Hopefully it won't be as many years till we see each other again," she said.

As we disconnected, Faith smiled at me, then disappeared.

☼

Now that Paula and I had made amends, it was time for me to reach out to another friend.

I kicked off my shoes and laid on the sofa, tucking the sunflower quilt around me. I closed my eyes, took a few relaxing breaths and drifted into the lucid realms.

I was again in the hovercraft, traveling down the highway with my three astral friends.

"Hi Jennie," Reno said, "don't look..."

"I know you're going to tell me to not look at the hag," I said.

"I'm glad you remembered," Reno said.

I patted Mitch's arm and said, "Still can't get the fear of her out of your system?"

"No, I can't," he said.

"It's not his fault, Jennie," Juliet said. "Stop picking on him!"

"I'm not, Juliet, I'm here to help him," I said to her. Then to Mitch I said, "You can get past this fear if you're willing."

"I am willing, but how?" Mitch said.

"We'll face her together," I said.

Juliet said, “No way am I getting tossed, dropped and dunked again!”

“You won’t have to, Juliet, if you and Reno leave now.” Juliet and Reno vanished leaving me alone with Mitch. I looked out the side window and said, “There she is, right on time.”

The hag stood on the median and with a wave of her hand our vehicle raised skyward. I grabbed Mitch’s hand as the car shook then flipped over. Mitch and I tumbled out, and I kept hold of his hand as we dropped into the lake and sank toward the abyss.

We swam to the surface, and I pointed toward shore. “Swim over there,” I said.

When we crawled up onto the lawn I looked for Bella’s Star, but she wasn’t there.

“Where are we? What are we doing here?” Mitch said.

“We are about to face your hag.”

“No, I can’t! I’m too afraid of her!”

“The only way to get past this fear is to face it. But don’t fret, I’ll be with you the whole time. Now do as I say and she won’t scare you anymore. Come on,” I said, and led him to the cottage.

We ran up the steps and when I knocked on the door, it swung open. We walked inside and the hag watched as we took a seat by the fireplace.

Mitch started trembling at the sight of her, and I said, “It’s going to be all right.”

“You again!” she said as she paced before Mitch. “What do you want from me?”

“What do you mean?” he said.

She stopped pacing and stared at him. “Why do you keep conjuring me?” she said.

“I’m not conjuring you,” he said.

“Yes, you are! Why do you keep bringing me round?”

“But I wouldn’t do that, you scare the hell out of me!” he said.

“I do?” she said as she stepped closer.

“Look more closely at her,” I said to him.

“What? Why?” he said.

"Just do it," I said.

He did so, and said, "It's all makeup and effects!"

The hag nodded, then transformed into the lovely actress.

"Who are you?" Mitch said.

She smiled and said, "I'm your hag."

"But you can't be," he said. "You look nothing like her."

"Well, thank you! But what you have been seeing is what you've been fearing, not reality."

"But who is the hag?" he said.

"I played her in a movie years ago. You watched it as a child and I guess my portrayal was a bit too much for your young mind. I'm sorry I caused your fear, but I'm here to help you release it now."

"Why you're not scary at all," he said. "You're beautiful."

She quickly morphed into the hag then back into the actress again, and winked at him. "You see," she said, "most fear has no substance. What is that saying?"

"Fear is false evidence appearing real?" I said.

"Yes, that's it," she said.

"Am I done with the nightmares, too?" he said.

"You're free if you want to be," she said.

"It's as simple as that?" he said.

"Yes, change your thoughts to change your results. It's just a matter of changing your mind," she said.

He nodded and smiled. "I believe I can do that! Thanks," he said to her, "and thank you, Jennie."

CHAPTER THIRTY-FOUR

JAKE WAS READY to leave for Kate's by the time I got home from work. I dashed into the house to grab the spoons I had bought at a thrift store, and we were on our way.

When we arrived at Kate's house, Jake rang the doorbell. Lola and Evan opened the door, and in unison said, "Hi, Nana. Hi, Papa." I found their calling him Papa endearing; and Jake liked it too.

We hugged the children, and Jake said to Lola, "Your repairman's here, my Princess."

Lola spun around and giggled with delight that he had noticed her tiara.

Evan pointed at his toy tool belt and said, "I'm gonna help you, Papa."

"Oh boy," Jake said.

Kate came in from the kitchen, and said, "I really appreciate your help, Jake."

"Don't thank me, yet," he said, and walked to the laundry room with Evan at his heels.

"You want to meet my friend, Nana?" Lola asked as she pulled my hand toward her bedroom.

"Is someone in your room?" I asked.

"So she tells me," Kate said as we followed Lola to her bedroom. "It's either a ghost or her imagination."

I stepped into the center of the room, and turned slowly. At the far corner was a presence, and I said, "Hello there."

"You see her, Nana?"

"I sense her."

"You do?" Kate said.

I nodded as the spirit materialized, and I said, "And I see her now too."

The spirit of the young girl looked at me, and said, "You can see me?"

"Yes, what's your name?"

"Helga," she said.

"Nice to meet you, Helga."

Helga sat next to Lola as she played with her dolls.

"She used to live here, Nana, and they had horses," Lola said.

"Oh?" I said, as a vision of a homestead appeared where Kate's house now stood. "Helga, my daughter's home is here now," I said.

"She knows, Nana," Lola said, "I've told her."

Helga looked off to the side as if someone was calling to her. "I'm coming, Pa," she said, and disappeared.

"Helga went home again," Lola said with a shrug. "She comes and goes."

"Who is she?" Kate asked.

"I sense she lived on a ranch that was located here a long time ago."

"Helga had dogs and cats, too," Lola said.

Kate sighed, and said, "Lola's been nagging me to get a dog."

I saw a vision of a dog and said, "It's brown and white, perhaps a Spaniel?"

Kate sighed again and said, "I hope it's not any time soon."

"When we get our dog, Mommy, can we name him Pal?"

"We'll see," Kate said. "Now let's check on how the men are doing with the washing machine."

"I'm staying here," Lola said.

"Okay. I'll call you when supper's ready," Kate said.

As we left Lola's room I whispered to Kate, "Be thankful she's not asking for a horse."

Kate cringed, then said, "I wasn't sure what to do about her invisible friend, and she also claims to talk to Brad."

"It's possible she's talking to her father."

"So I guess I have you to thank for her Gifts?" Kate said, then smiled.

"Can I have my present too, Nana?" Evan asked.

I looked down at my grandson standing in the doorway to the laundry room, holding a screwdriver. "What present is that, Evan?"

"Mommy thanked you for Lola's gift. What did you bring me?"

I pulled a dollar from my purse and said, "I brought you this."

"Thanks!" Evan said, and stuffed it in his pocket.

"He stuffs everything in his pockets." Kate said, "I'm always afraid to reach in his pockets for what I'll find when doing laundry."

"It's what boys do," I said, "Nathan was the same way."

We followed Evan into the laundry room, and I asked Jake, "How are you doing?"

Jake reached into the washer and said, "I think I just found your problem."

Kate said, "Oh? What was it?"

He pulled something out of the machine and said, "This. It was jammed under the agitator and not letting it spin."

We all looked at the plastic cowboy, then at Evan.

My grandson shrugged and said, "It was dirty."

"Next time your toys need cleaning, I'll do it," Kate said.

"Okay," Evan said as he took the toy from Jake.

"The washer should be okay now," Jake said. "Throw a load in while we eat and if there's still a problem, I can change the belt."

"Thank you, Jake," Kate said.

"Not a problem," he said.

"Well listen to you! Sounds like you know what you're talking about," I said. "Jammed agitator? A new belt? What's with the lingo?"

"I have Tom on speed dial," he said, and smiled.

☼

During dinner I told the children about Bella's Star.

"I'd like to ride Star," Evan said.

"You can't," Lola said.

"Why not?" Evan said.

"Cause only girls can ride Star," Lola said.

"No! Mom, Lola said..."

"I heard her, Evan, stop yelling," Kate said. "If we ever meet Star, I'm sure you can both ride her."

☼

After dinner I said, "I've brought something for us all to try."

"What is it, Nana?" Evan asked.

"You'll find out in a minute," I said as Kate and I cleared the table.

I set the spoons on the tablecloth. Evan looked at them and said, "Huh? Spoons?"

"Yes, we're going to play with them," I said.

Evan giggled and said, "Oh, Nana, we're not supposed to play with spoons. Right, Mommy?"

"Not usually," Kate said.

"But these are special spoons," I said.

"No, they aren't," Lola said, and ran to her room.

"Are they magic spoons?" Evan asked. "What do they do?"

"They twist and bend," I said.

"They do? How?" Evan said.

"You hold it with both hands like this," I said demonstrating to him. "Then you feel happy about something you've accomplished."

"Accomplished? What's that mean?" he said.

"Well, never mind that, just feel happy and imagine it bending as you say out loud, Bend! Bend! Bend!"

Evan picked up the spoon, held it in his hand, smiled with enthusiasm, and said, "Bend!" And it did!

"How did you do that?" I asked him.

He shrugged. "I don't know," he said, and bent another.

"How are you doing that?" I asked.

"Did I do something wrong, Nana? I thought you wanted me to bend it," he said.

"No, you're not in trouble," I said.

"Okay," he said and tossed the spoon on the table. "I'm going to watch TV."

Kate, Jake and I sat around the table, trying to bend our spoons with no luck. I tried a different spoon with no success. My palms were getting sore from pressing the hard metal.

"How does he do it?" I said.

"He doesn't doubt it," Kate said. "At Karate class recently, he had to break wood with his hand. The instructor said to him, 'Stop fearing the wood' as he pulled the stack away from him several times. But his instructor must have seen something change in Evan's expression, because then he held it in place and Evan broke it."

"That's how he bent the spoons tonight," Jake said. "He doesn't think he can't."

We all admired the child's confidence. He didn't wrestle with the spoon, or struggle with doubt. He just bent it, no big deal.

"Evan," I called to him in the living room, "will you come here, please?"

Evan ran up to me, and said, "What Nana?"

"Will you help me?"

He shrugged.

I held my spoon with both hands and said, "Can you place your hands on top of mine and help me bend my spoon?"

He nodded and placed his small hands on top of mine. I tried to mirror his smile, confidence and enthusiasm as together we said, "Bend, bend, bend!"

At first nothing happened, then I felt a slight give in the metal.

"Why did you stop, Nana?" he asked.

"Sorry, let's try again," I said. Again I held the spoon with his hands on top of mine. Together we said, "Bend, bend, bend!" and the handle bent in half!

"See Nana, you can do it too," he said.

"Thank you, Evan," I said, and gave him a hug.

"You're welcome," he said, and ran back to the television.

I picked up another spoon and now that I knew what the 'give' felt like, I was able to replicate my success.

☼

Back at our house, I tossed my purse on the bed and the original spoon from Sara's class fell out. I picked up the spoon and recalled Evan's enthusiasm and confidence as I studied it. I rubbed the silver handle and recalled Sara's asking us to think of a success.

At the time, my mind went blank. But now I thought of my store. My dream becoming a reality, an accomplishment. And I recalled how it felt bending the spoon tonight with Evan.

As I held that feeling of success and expectation, I said, "Bend! Bend! Bend!" And it did so easily.

And I realized that bending spoons was a simple task, but not an easy one. It's having the belief and enthusiasm of a child. Once you accomplish it, you know it can be done. But to do it, you must not doubt it. You must assume success, believing it will happen.

And then belief turns into the stronger vibration of knowing. When you know it, you feel it, you own it.

So it takes confidence, expectation, and belief to achieve. You must assume it first, know it is so.

This wasn't about spoons, but life. It's about core beliefs, it's about trust, it's about knowing.... it's about faith.

If you enjoyed this book, please tell your friends. And be sure to visit my website. When you *join the list* you'll be among the first to get updates about this Series, other publications and special offers.

Thank you ♥,
Lynn

http://www.LynnThomas.info/more

About the Author

Lynn Thomas is a nationally published and award winning author who discovered her love of writing while in childhood. Her paternal grandmother helped ignite her imagination with her story-telling and classic rhyming songs. And Lynn penned poems, songs and stories with her mother. And while she loves to write on a variety of topics, Lynn most enjoys creating inspiring entertainment for her readers.